BRIDGE
TO
OBLIVION

Henry Hoffman

Martin Sisters Publishing

Published by

Ivy House Books, a division of Martin Sisters Publishing, LLC

www.martinsisterspublishing.com

Copyright © 2011 by Henry Hoffman

ISBN: 978-1-937273-19-4

Fiction

Printed in the United States of America
Martin Sisters Publishing, LLC

DEDICATION

To Cheryl, Gratia, Barbara, Ann, Betty, and Merrill—friends for
all seasons.

~

Special thanks go to Barbara Beattie and Susan Sipal for their help
in the preparation of the manuscript.

As you from crimes would pardoned be,

Let your indulgence set me free.

(spoken by Prospero)
~ William Shakespeare, The Tempest

Fiction/Mystery

An imprint of Martin Sisters Publishing, LLC

PROLOGUE

~ *May 9, 1980*

Given a choice between her fear of flying and her fear of heights, she chose to keep her feet to the ground and take the bus to Miami. A car was out of the question. Traveling alone on the open road for long distances was not to her liking. In the end the bus was a compromise, a way for her to agree to her husband's request to represent him on the trip.

"I've seen much worse," said the old man camped in the seat next to her. He spoke in a breathy voice, angling his spindly frame for a better look at the vehicle's interior. "Yeah, it sure beats riding with chickens."

She ignored his overture. Unfortunately, it didn't prevent him from carrying on.

"Last bus I rode was down in Peru. It ran between villages up in the mountains. Visitors called it the poultry express. All you saw on board were people shuttling their crates full of cackling hens to and from the local market. Some even stuck a rooster in with their hens," he chortled, his shoulders hunching up and down. "Cripes, you never heard such a racket much less smelled one — had my head out the window for the entire ride to keep from puking. Problem was we were traveling these hairpin curves and I ended up staring down the face of one steep cliff after another. I swear we were no more than this far from the road's edge," he said, holding his gnarled hands close apart. "It's a wonder I lived to see this day."

She leaned her head back against the seat, turning her eyes to the window to signal her indifference.

He followed her gaze. "Looks like some rough weather's headed this way."

At least he didn't reek of alcohol, or tobacco smoke, or something worse, she thought, though the stained fisherman's hat on his head looked as if it had weathered some nasty experiences. To her relief, he was soon asleep. A temporary respite at best for she fully expected to have his head resting on her shoulder before the trip was half over. They had reached the long approach to the Sunshine Skyway Bridge and like the old man observed, the bad stuff was moving in. Large drops of rain began to splatter the bus's windshield, prompting the driver, a meaty-faced man with the look of an out-of-shape wrestler, to flip on the wipers.

As much as she and her husband would have liked it otherwise, the Miami event could not be ignored. An in-law was staging a weekend family gathering to celebrate a twenty-fifth wedding anniversary. To her husband's dismay, he was unable to accompany her due to a last-minute office emergency. At first, she was reluctant to take on the assignment due to a pressing circumstance on her own side of the family. Her younger sister recently had relocated to Tampa and was relying on her to ferry her around town until she was able to raise enough funds to purchase a car. "Don't worry, I'll see to it she has transportation," her husband had assured her. Still, the wife of a man of his position having to travel clear across the state on a bus did not sit well with her. "Sit down, Michael!" snapped a woman several seats behind her. A young boy was sprinting up and down the aisle, his little arms and long, blond locks flailing about. "You're bothering the driver."

By the time the bus cleared the toll station and started the precipitous climb to the bridge's summit, the winds had strengthened, kicking up a heavy chop on the bay. In the distance, the outline of the towering span was still visible, set against a bank of thunderclouds pulsating purple with bolts of lightning. She comforted herself with the thought she easily could have been up in the air in the center of the turbulence. Her husband had checked the airline schedules, discovering there was a morning flight leaving at nearly the same time the bus was due to depart. Looking out at the thickened sky, she imagined what it must be like for a pilot to navigate through such conditions.

*

"Better post a lookout on the bow," the harbor pilot instructed the captain as he prepared to maneuver his freighter, a ship the length of two football fields, beneath the Sunshine Skyway and into Tampa Bay. A light drizzle had quickly turned to a steady rain, and from the cast of the sky, conditions were about to worsen.

As the storm mounted, the pilot checked the ship's radar, which provided him a clear view of the buoys guiding him through the narrow shipping channel. A little more than a mile removed from the bay's entrance, he made radio contact with an outbound oil tanker approaching from two miles east of the bridge. Based on their present courses and speed, he calculated the tanker would reach the span before his arrival.

In short order, the wind and rain dramatically intensified, knocking the radar screen to a solid yellow and leaving him without reference to the buoys. He knew at once the ship was in serious difficulty. Empty of cargo and riding high on the waves, he considered his options. His initial instinct was to turn the ship hard to port. However, he first needed to contact the tanker headed in his direction. Executing a hard turn would take him across the outbound ship's path, raising the risk of a catastrophic collision.

An instant later he was back on the phone to the tanker.

"Captain? Do you read me? Do you read me?" he shouted above the wailing winds, receiving nothing but the crack of static in return.

Quickly, he considered his second option, to turn starboard, taking the ship into a spoils area. To do so he would have to steer the vessel broadside to the wind and risk losing total control of the ship. His final option, to drag the freighter to a halt by reversing its engines and dropping anchor, he immediately dismissed, since there was virtually no possibility of the vessel coming to a stop before it struck the span.

Standing on the ship's bridge, he squinted into the fury toward the direction of the dark swirls of clouds. Close by, the ghost-like image of the span rose into view, an unwelcome apparition jolting him to the realization that time and circumstance had joined to draw him into a convulsion of sea and sky he had no chance of escaping. Left to his own instincts and the whims of the winds, he did the only prudent thing, and aimed the laboring vessel toward the gap between the two main piers of the bridge.

*

Her seatmate started to snore, bobbing his head up and down to the cycle of grunts. She asked herself how anyone could sleep under these conditions. Not only was the squall lashing the windshield, rendering the bus's wipers useless, it also was rocking the vehicle's undercarriage with repeated uppercuts of wind.

She turned to see two smooching teenagers sitting in the row across from her postpone their dallying to join the ranks of the concerned, pressing their faces side by side against the window to view the torrent.

She looked to the driver for reassurance. He appeared to be the kind of man who had seen it all, though his face at the moment was drained of color. She caught him glancing at the rearview mirror, checking on his passengers who were stirring to the storm's onslaught. He was driving blind, she realized, gripping the edge of her seat.

"Folks, we're going through a little rough weather here," he called out in a robust voice. "Should be through it shortly."

If anywhere other than on the bridge, she was sure he would have pulled to the side of the road by now to wait it out. She checked her handbag for her medicine, believing for an instant she had left it behind. She breathed a sigh of relief when her probing fingers found the bottle.

The snorts emanating from the gaping mouth of the old man next to her grew louder, as the whirr of the bus's tires suddenly modulated to a low drumming sound, momentarily startling her. They had reached the metal grating portion of the span. Continually puzzled at why anyone would build the Skyway with a portion of roadbed through which you could see the waters far

8

below, was now, in some ways, a relief. A minute more of having to endure the washboard effect and they would be back on normal ground, heading off the bridge onto the level highway.

Eyes fixed to the window, she watched a pickup truck cruise past them into the murk ahead, its taillights burning like beacons. She followed them until they disappeared, dropping from sight like shooting stars from a blackened sky. Moments later, the vibration of the road beneath them abruptly ended, replaced for a split-second by a silent floating sensation, followed in turn by the sounds and images of tumbling bodies and baggage, as the bus cart-wheeled off the bridge into the abyss below, the sounds and images dissolving into nothingness.

HENRY HOFFMAN

CHAPTER ONE

~ *May 9, 1987*

All appeared in order for his first trip over the Skyway since its highly anticipated reopening, following five long years of construction. A starlit sky burned bright and traffic was light, leading him to believe an unobstructed night time spectacular awaited him on his crossing. In the distance he could see the span's soaring cables, shaped like twin sails, rising from the roadbed. Yet, as luck would have it, something other than a majestic view ended up grabbing his attention.

At first, he figured her for a jumper. What else could she be up to at this late hour, sitting alone on the bridge's railing in the full glare of the center span lights, looking forlorn? She stared hard into the moonlit waters of Tampa Bay over a hundred and fifty feet below.

Low on fuel and anxious to get home, still, he let his curiosity overcome his reluctance to get involved. He slowed his pickup, easing it onto the bridge's emergency lane not more than fifteen yards from her perch. Hopping from the truck, he quickly glanced around for another parked vehicle, occupied or otherwise, but none was in sight.

The smell of automobile exhaust hung in the air as he crossed the lane, dodging motorists who continued to whisk by, a few slowing to gape at the lone woman before pressing on.

His initial thought on approaching her was to ask himself why a woman who looked like that would be bent on such an act.

"Yo, baby...baby!" shouted a youth from a passing van filled with late-night revelers.

As if prompted, the woman immediately rose to her feet on top of the waist-high railing, momentarily freezing him.

"Ma'am, do you need help?" he asked from a discreet distance.

She ignored him, keeping her attention fixed on the waters below.

Searching for words, he mindlessly looked out at the circle of lights formed by surrounding bay front communities, glittering in the night like a jeweled necklace. Amid the circle appeared a tiny cluster of other orbs...red, green, and white...navigational lights coming from a small inbound cruise ship inching toward port. Afar, more lights in slow movement, from an airliner on its final approach to Tampa International.

He returned his attention to her. "Ma'am...ma'am?" he called out, mustering as much calm in his voice as he could.

She slowly swung her head in his direction, her windblown raven hair wrapping across her lower face like a veil, framing violet eyes as close to empty as his gas tank.

"I was just headed home to my wife and kids," he said, tossing truth to the wind. "How about you? Do you have a family...children?"

She held his gaze for what seemed minutes. By now one of the bridge's remote cameras was trained on them, he hoped. Surely, they would not be mistaken for a couple of careless thrill-seekers.

Nearby, a truck backfired, distracting neither.

"I hope she understands. It's where I belong," she finally said in a grave voice.

He nodded as though he understood.

For an instant he felt a flicker of hope, having snared her attention. A second look into her lifeless eyes, however, told him the hope was his, not hers. He reached out a helping hand, more in desperation than confidence, at the same time edging ahead for a pounce and grab, if necessary.

"Would you like to..." he said and stopped.

As if riled by his intervention, a fresh gust of wind lifted from the sea and rushed across the Skyway's surface, pressing at his back before nudging the woman forward from her perch.

He bolted toward her and in one fell swoop reached across the barrier to grab at a trailing arm. Instead, he snatched a hand. A critical miss, for in the same breath he felt the pass of her palm over his as she slipped finger by finger from his tenuous grasp. His heart lurched to his throat as he followed the tumbling figure, silhouetted against the reflected moonlight until it was swallowed by the darkness below. He listened for a splash before realizing the futility of it. Somebody's wife, daughter or sister was all he could think of, at once attempting to absorb what had happened while contemplating the transfer of familial pain to come.

He looked over his shoulder. The wail of a distant siren, followed by a second, commanded his attention. Somebody must have finally alerted the authorities to what was transpiring. Soon, the first responders arrived, angling their vehicles along the rail and in the emergency lane. Before long the area resembled a nighttime movie set with rotating overhead lights, spotlights, headlights, and flashlights beaming every which way, as crews scurried about the scene.

The only one missing was the lead character in the drama.

*

"The Marine Patrol has been notified," a burly guy crammed into a tan sheriff deputy's uniform informed him in a thick voice. "Chances are she didn't survive the fall.

They seldom do. It's like hitting a brick wall at sixty miles per hour. And if the collision doesn't finish them off, the currents do.

"What did you say your name was?" he continued, putting pen to paper.

"Adam Fraley."

"How old are you, Mr. Fraley?"

"Twenty-six."

"What kind of work do you do?"

"I'm a student at Live Oak Community College," he replied, adding that he also worked part-time, lest the guy think he was a professional student.

"And where do you work?" he asked, appearing bored with the routine.

"Peterson's Private Investigations. I just started a while back."

"Pete Peterson?"

"Yes," he answered, bringing a half smile to the deputy's chunky face.

"Okay, Adam, tell me what you saw."

He related how he saw the woman sitting alone on the rail on his approach, how she appeared to be in some sort of mental distress, how he decided to intervene and ask if she needed help, how she paid little heed to him, and how the wind seemed to grant her wish by nudging her off the bridge.

"An assisted suicide," the deputy cracked.

"I suppose you could call it that," he replied, annoyed with the remark.

"Can you give me a description of her?"

"Very attractive," he said, wishing he had left out the very part as soon as he saw the half smile reappear on the deputy's face. "Five-six or so...slender...long black hair...about my age give or take a couple of years...hard to say."

"How was she dressed?"

"Yellow blouse...long beige skirt...sandals."

"Did she have a handbag with her?"

"Yes, come to think of it, she was carrying one."

"Did you know this woman, Mr. Fraley?"

"No, never saw her before."

The deputy flipped a page of his notepad. "You sure about that?"

"Yes, I'm sure."

"Have any idea how she got here?

"No."

He realized the risk of playing the Good Samaritan role and its attendant no-good-deed-goes-unpunished rule. For sure, he would be checked for any kind of past relationship with the woman, not to mention placed in jeopardy for lawsuits from suspicious friends or family members charging negligence. Hell, even the assisted suicide notion, as ridiculous as it was, would not be outside an investigator's scope.

"Did she say..."

Another deputy abruptly handed a mobile phone to his inquisitor, interrupting the questioning. "Call for you."

"Olivo," the burly one barked into the phone, attempting to cradle it in one hand while scribbling with the other. "Yeah...right...a jumper...white female...a marine patrol unit is out searching now...one witness...says he didn't know her...says she didn't say much...says he works part time for Pete Peterson, the PI...describe him? White male...twenty-six...six two maybe...medium build...brown hair...close cropped...yes...no...no...okay.

"My commander," the deputy said, handing the phone back to his colleague.

"Why did he ask for my description?" he dared to ask.

"You know how law enforcement is, or maybe you don't. A description has to go with every name. There's always that surprise connection that might pop up. Okay, what was it she said to you?" he asked, checking his notes.

"She said 'I hope she understands. It's where I belong.'"

"Have any idea what she meant by that?"

"No idea."

"Notice any vehicle pulling away from the scene as you arrived?"

"No."

"Anything else you can tell me?"

He paused before answering. "No, nothing else to tell; it happened so quick."

"Yeah, some go fast. Some take their time."

The deputy clicked his pen, slipped it into his shirt pocket, closed his notepad, flexed his stubby fingers, and let out a deep breath.

"Okay, if need be, we will be getting in touch with you."

"I'm free to go?"

"Free to go."

He returned to his truck and his second-guessing. Did he spook her? Did she see through his lie about having a family? Was it the right thing to ask if she had one? Should he have driven on by and let someone else handle the situation?

He fired up his pickup and again joined the thinning flow of bridge traffic. It was now past midnight and he still had a gas station to find. He rolled up his windows to ward off the smell of rotting fish and seaweed carried in by the gulf breezes. The red tide forecasted to move down the coast had reached the bay area, he surmised, the foul odor bringing to mind the image of lifeless sea creatures washing up against the shore.

If only he could as easily ward off the image of her, a striking presence one moment, a burning memory the next.

CHAPTER TWO

"Would you have played the Good Samaritan if she had been one of those full-figured women?"

"Do I have to answer that?" he asked in return.

"You just did," cracked his boss, eyeing him from across the new solid oak desk he purchased a few months ago to coincide with the arrival of his new employee.

He learned early on the key to Pete Peterson's success. The guy had the knack for sizing up people in a moment's time. He just as easily could have been a personnel or jury selection specialist as a private investigator. When he dared to tell him so, the response was typical, if not entirely accurate. "You're only saying that because I hired you."

When he first saw the ad in the paper for part-time help at Peterson's firm he jumped at the opportunity. Here he was, fresh out of the military and in pursuit of a degree in criminal science. Now, he was being offered a chance to simultaneously gather some field experience and a little cash as well. The timing couldn't have been better. It was as good as an apprenticeship.

"Who was the cop covering the case?" Peterson asked.

"A guy by the name of Olivo."

"Don't know him."

"He gave a description of me to his boss over the phone. I thought that was a little strange."

"Cops have to cover all the bases, not to mention their backsides. The guy on the other end of the line may have had somebody in mind, maybe someone else who was spotted in the vicinity earlier in the day. There are those who hang around rest stops, you know."

"I don't hang around rest stops unless I need a rest."

"That's what they all say."

Adam shook his head in a dismissive gesture. "I'll never forget the look on her face," he said, redirecting their chitchat to the jumper. "It reminded me of what we were discussing in our Shakespeare class the other day...what was said about Lucrece."

"You're taking a course in Shakespeare?"

"Beginning Shakespeare...it's an elective they're letting me take."

"What else you taking?" Peterson asked, appearing a little dumbfounded.

"Intro to Criminology...Research Methods in Criminal Science...English Comp...and History and Principles of Journalism."

"You're not going to turn into an intellectual on me and start questioning every move I make, are you?"

"That's a bad thing?"

"It is if you can't accept authority. Intellectuals are to be listened to, not given control, in case you didn't know."

"I don't think the courses I'm taking will qualify me as an intellectual."

"Whatever happened to Fundamentals of Tailing a Guy?"

"That I'm going to learn from you."

Peterson leaned back in his tan leather chair. "Okay, who's Lucrece?" he asked, lacing his fingers behind his head

"A woman raped by an acquaintance."

"You're saying the jumping was the result of a rape?"

"No, not at all. Lucrece was having a hard time describing her feelings following the assault and says something like 'when more is felt than one has power to tell.' That's the way I felt looking at the jumper. She was feeling more than she had power to tell."

"Maybe you should have indicated it to her in some way."

"I didn't have time to indicate much of anything."

Peterson stood to shed his suit jacket, flinging it over the back of his chair. "How's the computer setup working?" he asked, nodding to the unit on the desk.

"Loaded and ready to go," he replied.

The machine was the main reason he was sitting at the desk in the first place. The previous office assistant was from the old school and rather than subject herself to the torment of learning a complicated new toy, she decided on early retirement.

"I've got all the reports loaded in and the Internet up and running," he said, shifting the monitor in his boss's direction.

"State of the art operation, don't you think?" Peterson said in half jest, keeping his attention on the computer screen while fingering the mouse.

"State of the art," he replied in kind.

In truth, the agency's one-room office stood as little more than a front operation. Located on the first floor of a ten-story terra cotta-tinged office building tucked between more grandiose downtown structures, it served its purpose, which was basically to provide a non-threatening atmosphere for potential clients. In keeping with his casual approach, Peterson decided to go with what he called a "tropic exotic" interior, meaning he scattered a few planters sprouting dracaenas in the corners, lined the peach paneled walls with paintings of baskets of fruit, and positioned a banana-plant lamp alongside a cluster of cognac-colored leather armchairs. Throw out the desk and you had the typical Florida reception room, which was appropriate, since most of the real business was conducted in Peterson's upscale midtown home, where clients could come and go without feeling embarrassed about patronizing the downtown locale. Furthermore, his wife of thirty years was at home to serve as insurance against one of the trade's occupational hazards…the highly charged atmosphere in which a victimized, vulnerable female is looking for some stability in her life and decides the private eye is the guy to provide it.

From day one his boss made clear to him their services were by appointment only. The guidelines were simple … first, don't do anything illegal … second, give top consideration to referrals from cops or companies … third, look for emotionally stable and financially solvent clients … fourth, seek cases calling for general surveillance or record searching only.

Peterson's scope of investigation had been much broader at one time, but as business grew so did the luxury of lowering the risk factors by tightening the criteria for taking on a case. His was essentially a business built on word of mouth, the mouths happening to belong to the lucrative set. Still, the phone book listings continued, not only to put a public face on the operation, but accommodate the occasional walk-in client as well.

"There was a guy called who said you did some work for his company — Jack Rogers — Rogers Electronics — employee background checks — ring a bell?"

"Yeah, couple of years ago…what did he want?" Peterson asked, continuing to work the mouse.

"It's personal this time. Says his daughter is going through a nasty divorce and custody battle. He wants to get the goods on the son-in-law. Says he's been cheating among other things. Now he's even hiding the family dog from her."

"No thanks…tell him my plate's full."

"What about a dating case. I had a woman call this morning who wants to check on this guy she's been seeing. She wants to know if he's hiding a wife. Same thing?"

"No, not the same at all. There's a light year's difference between the two. One's a domestic dispute situation…the kind the police hate getting dragged into. What usually happens is the police intervene and, presto, both the husband and wife end up turning on the cops. I've had my fill of those. The dating thing is different. Emotions are less vested, so the chance of fireworks is also less. You can handle that one, probably without leaving the office," he said. "But if so, don't forget travel expenses are part of the fee, especially if you end up in Bermuda."

Peterson rose and grabbed his suit jacket, slipping it over his narrow shoulders. He possessed a penchant for off-white suits, part of his tropical preference. As he was about to leave, he retrieved a comb from his inside pocket and carefully slicked back his silky gray hair to highlight a sharp face dominated by a prominent nose from which sloped drawn cheeks and chin.

"Pete, what did you make of the article on the jumper?"

"The one in *The Beacon*? Not much more than a filler piece, as I saw it."

"An unidentified woman from Ohio leaps to her death from the Skyway Bridge and the body is later recovered fifty yards from shore…end of story. And buried on page six."

"What about *The Gazette*? Did they have any better coverage or did you check it?" Peterson asked.

"Yes…also buried inside," he replied. "I'm debating whether to bring it up with my journalism professor. She's also an editor at *The Gazette*."

"What's there to debate?"

"She's a bit intimidating."

His boss chuckled. "You're in the wrong business, Adam, if you are easily intimidated."

"Maybe I have a lot to learn about journalism or else maybe I'm thinking it rates higher because I was a witness."

"It's a suicide, Adam. The media treats them in a sensitive manner, if you can believe it. It's come up in a few cases of mine. The rule seems to be if it's a private citizen doing it on private property, you don't run with it. If it's a public figure doing it on private property, you do run with it. If it's a private citizen doing it on public property, you split the difference—you don't make a big deal out of it—you mention it and leave the names out whenever possible, especially if the person is from out of town. Also, there's always the fear among media types the story might trigger other suicide attempts."

"So you think that will be the extent of their coverage?" Adam asked.

"Wouldn't surprise me. Did the broadcast media call you?"

"One of the TV stations reached me on my home phone the next night, but I just repeated what I told the police."

"Much too late and too little for their news cycle," Peterson said.

"Puzzling," he said, drumming his fingers on the desk. "Why would a woman from Ohio be leaping from a bridge in Florida?"

"If you want to get the lowdown, why don't you get yourself a copy of the sheriff's report?"

"Down the street?"

"Yes. Remember, though, this one's on your own time and expense," he said, whistling a happy tune on his way out the door.

*

Adam picked up a copy of the sheriff's report on his way home, deciding to postpone reading it until later. He first had to meet with his landlady, a chubby woman by the name of Wanda who continually chugged about the grounds of the complex, but usually with a big smile etched on her moon face. They were scheduled to go over some maintenance problems he was having.

Home was a studio apartment in an off-campus housing district located on a block made up mostly of old frat and sorority houses featuring the occasional frayed couch on the porch. He considered his studio one grade up from military barracks life. After all, it did boast a tiny kitchen with a gas stove and midget fridge. Squeezed into the remaining space was a pull-down bed and rented furniture, all resting on a wood floor that had seen enough foot traffic to fill a coliseum a couple of times over. Bathroom and laundry facilities were of the communal type, centered down a connecting hallway.

With Wanda in tow, he pointed out the problems, including two very stubborn window frames, a couple of loose doorknobs, and a leaky faucet. The plumbing problem was particularly annoying. The drone of airplanes or the rumbles of trains he could bear. Dripping, on the other hand, was capable of keeping him up an entire night.

On leaving, Wanda promised the problems would be taken care of within the week. No sooner was she out the door than he was stretched out on the couch with the sheriff's report in hand.

Charlene Gibbs was her name and Hidden Valley, Ohio, her hometown. They were the only items of note. The rest was a rehash of what appeared in the paper, except for a reference to an Adam Fraley who witnessed the jump.

"It's where I belong," he repeated to himself, laying aside the report. Charlene Gibbs of Hidden Valley, Ohio, believed she belonged at the bottom of Tampa Bay. And why should he care? The question weighed on him through his afternoon and evening classes, calling for his attention like a restless child bidding for a mother's ear. His was the last face she saw, the last face she spoke to. Could that be reason enough to care?

*

"At least you got yourself a name and city," Peterson said, interrupting his scanning of the computer screen to take a swig of bottled water.

Adam relegated the matter of the police report to the end of his briefing, as if it was an afterthought. The last thing he wanted to do was make it appear he was playing with a different set of priorities.

"Is your curiosity now satisfied?" his boss asked.

"Not entirely," he replied. "There's still the question of why she felt she belonged at the bottom of the bay.

"She may not have meant Tampa Bay, maybe it was the hereafter she was referring to when she said 'it's where I belong'.

You ever think of that? So far, you seem to have more emotion than evidence invested in this incident," he said, clicking the print command.

"Is this one of those up-front, lost-cause cases you were warning me about?"

"Did you get the new phone book yet?" Peterson asked, ignoring his question.

"Yeah...sure did," he said, retrieving it from a desk drawer.

"May...1987," his boss said, pointing to the cover. "That's it." He took the book and flipped through the pages. "Gibbs...Gibbs...here we go...nope, no Charlene Gibbs...let's see...C. Gibbs...okay."

He picked up the phone and dialed the number his finger landed on.

Adam flashed him a quizzical look. "She's from out of town...remember?"

Peterson placed his free hand over his mouth and yawned. "Listen...nearly everyone in these parts is from somewhere else. You ask somebody on the street where they are from and they announce another town and state. How do you think Florida managed to pass Ohio in population? It's because everyone up there is moving down here." He plopped the phone back into the receiver. "Line disconnected...interesting. Let me see that crisscross directory."

He slid the directory across the desk and immediately his boss began to search the address section of the book.

"The street address for C. Gibbs is shown as the Mid-Town Apartments," he said, dialing a number. "God, it's hot in here. Did you check on the air?"

"There's a crew coming in tomorrow to take a look at it, so says the building superintendent."

"Yes...I am trying to locate a person by the name of Charlene Gibbs and I can't seem to reach her," he said into the phone. "Can you tell me if she still...oh...okay...no longer lives there."

Peterson cocked an eye across the desk. "Did she leave a forwarding address or phone number where she could be reached? Oh, you don't give out that kind of information. Well, this is her dentist's office and we needed to contact her regarding an appointment...oh...oh...sorry to hear that...sudden was it...how did it happen, if you don't mind me asking...that's all you know...okay, thanks for the information."

He hung up the phone and paused to again rinse his throat with water, his large Adam's apple pulsating with each gulp. He let out a deep breath when finished.

"Charlene Gibbs did live at the Mid-Town Apartments for two months. She was killed in an unfortunate incident, according to the manager, and no longer resides there," he said matter-of-factly, resting his bottle on the desk.

He wasn't sure which was the bigger disappointment, his stupidity in not checking the phone book or learning Charlene Gibbs had been a fellow Tampa resident after all.

"I guess that answers the question of why she chose the Skyway Bridge," Pete said, gulping another mouthful of water. "This gal must have made *some* impression on you. You might want to drop by the medical examiner's office and check the after-the-fall photos. They're sure to dampen your ardor."

He shrugged. "What does it matter now?"

"So your question has been answered?"

He nodded.

Peterson screwed the cap back on his bottle and headed for the door, pausing for a parting exchange.

"Now I have a question."

"What's that?"

"I said earlier everyone around here considers themselves as being from somewhere else. Well, that might be true for the man in the street, but the legal community sees it much differently, which raises another question. Why would the sheriff's report not list her local address?"

*

If not for the fact that the Mid-Town Apartments were within a stone's throw of his route home, he might have avoided the temptation and been home studying by now. Instead, he found himself facing the façade of a four-story red-brick complex from its scarred asphalt parking lot, debating whether to track down the manager or not. He was still mulling over the idea when he walked through the entranceway, stopping to scan the cluster of mailboxes embedded in the lobby wall. Only one was missing a name below it. Across the hall was the manager's office, the door closed. He knocked, somehow feeling an obligation to do so. To his relief there was no answer. What was the manager going to tell him that he hadn't already told Peterson?

He noted the apartment number of the mail slot with the missing name and climbed up a narrow concrete stairwell to the second floor; passing on the way a middle-aged male headed downward who paid him no heed. Entering a red-carpeted hallway, he heard a television set blaring from behind one of the closed doors. Halfway down the corridor he spotted the apartment number. Standing before the door he raised his fist, paused a moment, and knocked. There was no answer.

What the hell was he expecting—a vision of her standing in the opened doorway with the life back in her eyes and a smile on her face as she invited him in?

He left the building the same way he entered it, debating his actions. Crossing the parking lot he came upon a frail elderly woman walking the grounds like a wounded stork in high heels with her dog in tow. She wore an embroidered smocked dress and a facial expression too inviting to pass.

"May I ask what breed of dog is that, ma'am?"

"A Papillon," she said, reining in the pet.

"That's some set of ears he has," he said.

"Yes, but it doesn't matter. He seldom listens to me anyway," she said, loosening the leash as the dog launched into a happy feet routine.

He dropped to one knee to stroke the pet's lush white coat.

"Are you from this area?" she asked, brushing back strands of her unruly gray hair. "I haven't seen you around here before."

"No, I'm originally from Strawberry Hills, about an hour's drive north of here," he said, rising to his feet "My name is Adam Fraley, and yours?"

"Rosemary," she said straightforward. "You're now living in Tampa?"

"Yes."

"Why did you decide to leave home?"

"I joined the Air Force to see the world and the first place they sent me after basic training was to MacDill Air Force Base here in Tampa."

"Do you fly airplanes?"

"No, I worked on the ground during my entire stint. The one exception was when they flew me to boot camp in Texas. I spent the rest of my time in the Air Security Police."

"The police…oh. Do you have a family?"

"Just my parents who still live in Strawberry Hills."

A motorcyclist revving his engine several times wheeled into the parking lot, drowning the conversation.

She rolled her eyes, as the cyclist gave one last rev before shutting the vehicle down.

"I don't know what's becoming of this place," she said, clicking her tongue.

"Say, do you know if the manager is in today?"

"He comes and goes," she said in an offhanded manner.

"He's not in his office," Adam said. "Out to lunch, maybe?"

"Could be. He also manages another complex down the road owned by the same company. Why? Are you looking for an apartment?"

"No, I wanted to ask him about a woman who lived here…a lady by the name of Charlene Gibbs. Did you know her by chance?"

"This doesn't have anything to do with the Air Police, does it?" she asked, her face covered by concern.

"No...no. I'm no longer in the Air Force."

She eyed him carefully for a moment. "What a horrible thing to happen is all I can say."

"Then you did know her?" he asked, feigning surprise.

"Oh, I didn't know her personally, but I did run into her on occasion like I did with you. She was such a pretty young lady and nice too. She would always smile pleasantly, at least to me. Are you a friend of hers?"

"Only an acquaintance but it still came as a shock to me," he said.

She held her thought and shook her head. "In all honesty, other than the smiles she gave me, she did not seem all that happy."

"How's that?"

"Well, she always kept to herself. I didn't see her coming and going with anyone very often, other than this one fellow who sometimes stopped by to escort her out."

"A boyfriend maybe?"

"Could have been, though like I say, I didn't see her smiling much, other than at me."

"Not at the visitor?"

"No."

"Maybe they weren't social get-togethers?" he suggested.

"Possible, though they looked like they could have been a couple. Nowadays you never know."

She chuckled, touching her hand to her mouth. "Perhaps I shouldn't say this, but the man must have been a car salesman. Every time I saw him he was driving a different make of car."

"That right?"

"Yes...a nice one too. In fact, he didn't look like he belonged in this neighborhood at all," she said, casting a glance at the surroundings.

28

"Why so?" he asked, pleased the lady was starved for talk.

"For one thing, he was always wearing nice dress shirts and slacks," she said, her eyes giving him the quick once over, as if his jeans and T-shirt did not measure up.

"What about girlfriends?" he asked, pressing his luck.

"No...no girlfriends I know of," she said in a dismissive manner. "Anyway, that's about all I know. Like I said, she wasn't here that long. How about you? You say you were an acquaintance, yet I've never seen you around here."

"I was just dropping by on a business matter...nothing too important, but I do thank you for the information. I may stop back in a while to see if I can catch the manager in his office," he said, rethinking his interest in seeing him. He then stooped to give the Papillon a parting pat on the head before heading to his truck.

An hour later Adam was back at the complex and back staring at Charlene Gibbs' door, as if it magically would open at any moment. The manager was still out of his office, so he decided to stroll to the second level on the chance he might spot him wandering the floors. Prepared to leave, he instinctively reached out to twist the doorknob in a final goodbye effort, when he heard footsteps in the hallway.

"Are you the guy from Shepherd House?" barked a baby-faced guy with a bony shaved head, save for two faint lines of peach-fuzz eyebrows.

"Yes," he answered impulsively, hoping for an opening, though expecting an embarrassment.

"We'll be glad to get this placed cleaned out. You got your movers with you?"

"No, I wanted to stop by first to see what kind of manpower and truck capacity we would need."

The manager shoved a hand into his baggy jeans pocket and pulled out a set of keys, sticking one into the lock. "Some guy supposedly cleaned out the personal items," he said, swinging open the door and motioning him in. "It's normal procedure in these situations for some family member to rush in and clean out the embarrassing stuff."

"Who was it?" he casually asked.

"Not sure…some in-law, I was told. I'm just the assistant manager. The top guy is out checking on another complex."

On entering they were greeted by an interior of pinks and purples—light pink walls, light purple carpeting, and furniture upholstered in shades of pink and purple floral patterns. Also there to greet them was the clear yet indefinable scent of another person's personal living space.

"Doesn't look like there will be a lot to haul away," the manager said at first glance. "That entertainment center might be a load," he added, pointing to a black-paneled unit centered against one of the walls.

Clean and orderly, the unit exhibited a utilitarian look, like the renter had yet to decide whether it was a keeper by decorating it up with personal keepsakes and mementos. Either that or the in-law carted them all away. The only item resembling an heirloom was an antique wall clock, its pendulum still swinging to the correct time.

He was directing an eye to some framed black-and-white photos of woodland winter scenes mounted on the living room walls, when the manager called from the kitchen.

"Fridge is nearly empty except for some fruit. So are the cupboards," he said, between the sounds of cabinet doors opening and closing.

Moments later the manager rejoined him in the living room. "She must have believed in the ice-box diet," he said, munching on a banana.

Adam interrupted his gazing of photos to look at the guy incredulously.

"Well, it would have gone to waste," he pleaded, hoisting his heavy shoulders and half-eaten banana into the air.

"What's the ice-box diet?" he asked, turning his attention from the banana eater to the drawers of a small living room desk on top of which rested a vase filled with roses.

"Simple. You got nothing in the fridge—you got nothing in the tummy. Works every time," he said, the words coming from a man whose belly hung over his belt.

"You know, we're faced with this quite often in apartment work," the manager went on to say.

"Faced with what?" he asked absentmindedly.

"People dying suddenly and us having to arrange the disposal of their belongings. Some families believe in tossing everything out, thinking they're also tossing out the personal pain with the personal items."

Adam sauntered into the bedroom, followed by the manager, as well as a gnawing feeling that he was invading the privacy of the woman on the bridge. What was he looking for? Clues? And to what? He felt he was playing more the role of nosy neighbor than private investigator.

A large waterbed with a checkered lavender and white bedspread and two red velvet pillows caught his attention. Not a crease in them, he noted, raising the question of whether someone planning to take their own life would go to such lengths to make sure everything was left in perfect order. He recalled the account he read in the paper several years past of the elderly couple involved in a double suicide, who saw to it their house was in immaculate shape before carrying out their final act.

"Look at this—still full of clothes," the manager said, leaning his head into a walk-in closet. "Shoes lined up neatly, too," he added, backing his head out. "I guess the in-law didn't consider clothes personal possessions. My wife tells me her mother made it a point of saving some of her father's clothing following his passing so she could haul them out every year on their wedding anniversary to feel and sniff them. Ever hear of such a thing?"

Adam ignored the question, stepping back into the living room for a final look around.

31

"How soon do you expect your fellows will be able to get this place cleared?" the manager asked. "We'd like to put it back up for rent as soon as possible."

"Soon," he said on the way out the door, conscious he had taken a small step into Charlene Gibbs' past. Somehow, at least in his own mind, a posthumous bond had been formed between them, the nature of which he did not yet know. But because of it, a twinge of melancholy accompanied him home.

*

"Are you ready for your performance evaluation?"

Adam turned his eyes from the computer screen to his boss across the desk casually considering a form he held in front of him. The question took him by surprise. There had been no mention of performance evaluations during the orientation process, what little of it there was.

"Yes, performance evaluation," Peterson said, seeing the reaction on Adam's face. "According to the leader of a small business seminar I was roped into attending a while back, documentation is the key to developing a productive staff. You got to document, document, document, he kept repeating to us. Ever have one?"

"No," Adam replied. Have you ever given one?"

"Nope, but what better time to start than with a new employee on board?"

"You *had* an employee. Why didn't you start with her?"

"Her years put her beyond the evaluation process. I let her hang around so long she became entrenched. The gal was a bureaucracy of one who refused to budge from her set ways. The only thing finally to budge her was my decision to automate the place. Can't make the same mistake again. Therefore, I have decided to implement this performance review procedure, effective immediately. It provides me the grounds to fire you, if need be," he said, poking his grinning face out from behind the form.

"You don't need a document to send me packing, Pete. Simply

point me to the door whenever you feel the time has come."

"I think I'll make this an oral one," he said, continuing his scanning of the form.

"That's documenting?"

"It's not fair to spring a written one on you without notice. This will count as your three-month one," he said, twisting the desk calendar around to check the date. "The six-month one will be the written variety."

"If I make it that far," Adam said, leaning back in his chair with a bemused smile on his face as his boss continued to wing it.

"I've got my hopes for you," Peterson said, flipping to the next page of the document. "Let's see now. Planning and organizational skills—I'd say so far so good, already on a par with your predecessor. Knowledge of written policies and procedures..."

"We don't have written policies and procedures, at least none I have seen," he said, interrupting the flow.

Peterson again peeked from behind the document. "You're right, and that will be worthwhile assignment for you to undertake somewhere down the line," he said before proceeding. "Technical skills—it does look like you have the computer thing down. Interpersonal skills—got no complaints from the customers or neighbors thus far. Work habits—on time—meets deadlines. Safety—no trip and fall hazards I know of. Communication—keeps boss informed—good listener." Peterson peeled back another page. "Okay, now it asks for strengths and weaknesses. What do you think?"

"You asking for my opinion?"

"Self-evaluation is a critical component of any performance rating procedure, we were told. So, give me a strength and weakness. One each will do," he said, lowering the form.

"Loyal and impatient."

"I'd say level-headed and impatient."

"You have the final say."

Peterson glanced at the back page of the document. "Okay,

that's enough evaluating for now," he said, slipping the document into his briefcase and exchanging it for a map he proceeded to spread across the table. "Anything else going on?"

"There's a tenants' meeting Monday morning."

"Good, you can represent me," his boss replied, keeping his eyes on the map. "I've always believed in delegating responsibilities. Attending tenants' meetings is one of them. It's good to get out and mingle with the neighbors once in a while. They can come in handy at times. And by the way, tell the super these fluorescents in here are giving me headaches and ask why we can't replace them with soft track lighting?"

"I think they are more concerned with issues in the common areas, like putting up corkboards in the hallways."

"Yeah, I noticed one of them the other day," Peterson said, drawing his finger across the map. "Whose work is that?"

"I think it was the nail salon ladies. They're allowing customers to pin up their personal business cards and notices of events."

"Great."

"So what's our position on the matter?" he asked the top of his boss's head.

"We don't have one. How's that?" he said, scribbling a note. "I got to hand it to those nail gals. They are really into the marketing. Last year they were trying to convince me to let them station one of their people in here to provide our clients a complimentary manicure while they waited for their appointment. 'You ever see anybody in here waiting for an appointment?' I asked them."

"Management is also considering piping in music to the common areas—reggae maybe. That was the print shop guys' idea."

"As long as it's confined to the hallway. Music and the private investigation business don't go together. People aren't in the mood for it. They don't want relaxation. They want action, something to start them on the road to revenge."

"The other item is security. Apparently, there is still a lot of concern over a mugging in the hallway some time back. Do you recall it?"

Peterson lifted his eyes from the map and took a swig of water.

"It happened not long before you came on board. I was gone at the time but your predecessor said one of the print shop guys came running in here looking for me as if I was the cop on duty. The next day I was tempted to put up a sign on the door—'Call 911 in Case of an Emergency.'"

"We don't object to adding a security presence?"

"If they want to put us on a rent-a-cop patrol, it's fine with me, as long as it doesn't result in a hike in the rent," Peterson said, his face back into the map. "Ever been to Belize?"

"I haven't been out of the country," Adam said, his attention drawn to the map.

"Not even when you were in the Air Force?"

"Nope, I was confined to the states."

"Guarding buildings?"

"Buildings and people."

"Got a passport?"

"Nope."

"So much for overseas assignments. You need to get yourself one, especially living and working here in Florida. Getaways to the Caribbean and South America might be fun for others, but they are mostly work for us."

"Will do."

"This little piece of real estate is fast becoming a playground for the rich," he said, tracing Belize's borders with his finger.

"You planning a vacation?"

"No, this is strictly business. Does the name Rita Gordon ring a bell with you?"

"There was a Gordon Report I entered into the computer—a surveillance case if I remember right."

"Rita Gordon is a former cop. She took early retirement after getting married a few years ago. Her maiden name is Maroney.

Her husband Jack Gordon builds golf courses for a living. For the last year he's been traveling to Belize every week or so, supposedly on business. She suspects it may be monkey business."

"I thought we were staying away from the divorce stuff?"

"It hasn't reached divorce status yet. Besides, this is a special favor case. The Maroney name is a familiar one in local law enforcement circles, especially among the higher-ups. We've gotten some good referrals from them."

"You spending the weekend down there?"

"Yes, at the same resort where the golf course is going up."

"You play the game?"

"I could be this weekend for the first time in I don't know how long," Peterson said, attempting to refold the map back into its original shape. "I probably should hit the driving range before I go."

"Your wife believes your story?"

"Very funny, Fraley. How about you? Got a big weekend planned?" he asked, pocketing the crumpled map.

"I'm also headed out of town," he answered.

"Anyplace exciting as Belize?"

Adam paused, mindful of the reaction to come. "Hidden Valley, Ohio."

Peterson didn't hesitate. "How come that doesn't surprise me? Anything you can't do over the phone—your phone?"

"As you made clear to me, Pete, they still call it Private Eye and not Private Ear for a reason. I stopped by her apartment complex on the way home last night. A talkative neighbor said she had one male friend and no girlfriends as far as she knew. That's it as far as a social life."

"And?"

"And now I'm wondering who the *she* was that Charlene Gibbs referred to on the bridge."

"And the guy she was hanging out with you're not concerned about?"

"I'm guessing he was not in her final thoughts, though he may have had something to do with her being there.

"Okay, just don't tell me you're looking for closure. After twenty-five years in this business I can tell you this.. there is no such thing as closure when it comes to handling human tragedy. There's always a residue of guilt lying around somewhere."

Adam nodded, though unsure if it was closure he was after. He felt like the recipient of a private message intended for another and confused as to where and whom to deliver it to.

HENRY HOFFMAN

CHAPTER THREE

Hidden Valley was neither hidden nor a valley, as the surrounding terrain and approaching signpost indicated. He had spent nearly seven hours on the road, six of them to make it to the Kentucky border, where he found a motel to spend the night before setting out on the final leg of the trip.

The sign pointed him to a state road exit, which in turn fed him onto a tar and crushed stone road where another marker informed him he had another twenty-five miles to his destination.

Exchanging the grind of the interstate for the balm of the country road allowed him time to soak in the surroundings. The land took on a new cast, as the morning sun burned its way through an early morning fog to light a stretch of narrow highway as far as the eye could see. Off in the distance, whitewashed houses trimmed in blues and purples and bathed in sunlight rested on rolling hillsides carpeted by lush green grasses and wildflowers. A stranger to the seasons, he still could appreciate a northern spring at its zenith. If not for the groundhogs dashing into the middle of the road and lifting their heads to sniff the air in every direction before scampering from his way, he easily could have drifted into a transcendental state.

He lowered the pickup's windows and immediately the cab was filled with the rustle of leaves from passing stands of sycamore trees bordering the highway. Shortly, the top of a water tower appeared above the trees, signaling a town ahead. A city limits sign made it official...HIDDEN VALLEY...POPULATION 1542. Soon, the hillside white houses gave way to roadside white houses with big porches. They were followed in turn by several faded storefronts and an intersection marking the center of town.

He eased his truck through a flashing yellow light, wondering whether the intersection had ever merited a green-yellow-red signal. He recalled what Peterson said about the migration south of Ohio residents. From the looks of it, a goodly number of Hidden Valley's residents already had joined the exodus.

Crossing the intersection he came upon Molly's Kitchen, a small café with a chalkboard propped up out front announcing a breakfast special of sweet potato pancakes and bacon for $2.95. He pulled into the gravel parking lot, figuring Molly's was as good a place as any to launch his search without having to alert local authorities to his presence.

Entering the eatery he noted the interior, like the exterior, resembled a city diner more than a country café with its trolley car design and narrow interior aisle running between a counter with swivel stools and a succession of green vinyl booths.

A pony-tailed waitress with a friendly smile and coffee-stained apron stretched around her ample frame greeted him at the counter where he eyed a menu. "What can I get you, hon'?" she asked, pulling a writing pen from her hair.

Adam ordered the special and then settled back to listen to the loud banter of a group of old men in old overalls sitting in the booth behind him. Contributing to the clatter were the sporadic bursts of shorthand slang tossed by the waitress to the back of a cook who was busy working a steam-hissing grill behind an open service window. Occasionally, one of the men in the booth would get up and stroll behind the counter and help himself to a refill of coffee, as if it was part of the standard operating procedure. All the while a country and western tune emanating from a jukebox played above the din.

"Do you have a public phone?" Adam asked the waitress during one of her flybys.

"No phone," she said, pausing to take a single swipe at the counter.

"What about a phone book?"

"That we have," she said, reaching under the counter to pull out a chapbook and drop it before him.

It was similar to Strawberry Hill's directory, a spiral-bound notebook with a few typed white pages and no separate business listings. He checked under the name Gibbs and came up empty. There were no listings at all for a Gibbs. He considered running the name by the waitress but thought better of it, feeling it inappropriate at this point to bring up the dead woman's name.

"Is there a newspaper in this region?" he asked instead, confirming his stranger-in-town status.

"If you want to call it that," she replied, delivering his meal. "It's a weekly and won't be out till tomorrow."

"Do they have an office in town?"

"Hey Jake!" she called out in a gravel voice to one of the men in the booth. "Do you know where the *Weekly Courier's* office is located? This young fellow here wants to know."

The man jerked his head away from his buddies. "Sure do," he said. "It's over in Rocky Point. If you head back to the interstate and take the next exit north, you'll find it. The easier way is to continue down this road for about ten miles till you hit the intersection of state road 36. Hang a left and about twenty-five miles north you'll be in Rocky Point. You can't miss the *Courier's* office. It's right at the corner of the town's main intersection."

He nodded his appreciation, sped through the last bites of his soggy pancakes, and then headed out. Following the advice of the man in the booth, he took the back-roads route through more rolling farmland. The farther he traveled, however, the more he became aware of the doubt creeping into his head. He had witnessed a young woman leap to her death, and for no good reason, here he was, poking into her past, hundreds of miles north of where she ended her life. Surely, there were those who harbored a more personal interest in her plight, who cared more for her cause. Even a glimpse of the city limits sign of Rocky Point failed to quell his doubts.

As advised he found the newspaper's office at the corner of the town's main intersection. Stretched across its front window in stenciled yellow lettering were the words "The Weekly Courier." The storefront building was small enough to invite a knock on the door but instead he entered unannounced, stepping into a room not much larger than a wealthy man's walk-in closet. Sitting behind a cluttered desk, picking at a computer keyboard, was a stocky middle-aged man sporting a bad hairpiece, wrinkled white shirt, and dark blue tie twisted to the side like someone just tried to hang him with it.

"Yes, what can I do for you?" he asked without looking up from the monitor.

"Are you the editor?"

"I'm the editor, publisher, reporter, and sometimes the delivery boy," he said, shifting his attention from the monitor to stretch his hand across the desk. "Frank Morgan, and you are?"

"Adam Fraley."

"What is it I can do for you?"

"I'm in search of some information regarding a local matter and thought you might be able to help me," he said.

"Sure, have a seat," he said, motioning to a chair aside his desk. "What is it you're after?"

"What I'm after is some information on a local woman by the name of Charlene Gibbs who I understand died a sudden death recently."

"Charlene Gibbs," he said, repeating the name more as a

statement than a question. "Friend of yours?"

"A former acquaintance," he said, setting aside his witness role lest he quickly become the story. "I happened to be driving through this area and thought I'd check to see if it's true."

"Where you from?"

"Tampa, Florida."

"And you didn't hear of her death?"

"Very little. Apparently, there wasn't much mention of it in the Tampa paper or on the local news there, other than she jumped from a bridge."

"Your Sunshine Skyway Bridge to be exact," Morgan said. " Charlene was buried the other day over in Hidden Valley where she originally was from. I didn't know her personally, but it still came as a shock, considering the circumstances."

"I was just curious about the details…what might have led her to do it."

Morgan reached out and tapped the lever of a jellybean dispenser nearly buried in his piles of papers, releasing in his hand a few pieces of the candy. He tossed them toward his mouth, one missing and hitting the floor and rolling into a far corner where it finally spun to a stop.

"I don't have many details. As you can see this is a small operation," he said, motioning to the room with a sweep of his hand. "I mainly rely on a few local contacts for my information. In fact, I got wind of her death by way of our mortician who tipped me off her body was being transferred up here. As soon as I received the message, I was on the phone with the authorities down your way and was informed it was a simple suicide, if there is such a thing. From what I was told, the Skyway Bridge is a popular jumping off point…that right?"

"The old bridge certainly was," Adam answered. "What about family? Are any still around?"

"All gone…parents and sister."

"She had a sister?"

43

Morgan stared at him in amazement, like he was either a wayward time traveler from another century or else far less the acquaintance of Charlene than he claimed to be.

"Yes, she had a sister—an older one," he said. "Don't you remember the day the ship hit the stand? I think that's how it was referred to down in your region."

It was Adam's turn to look across the desk in amazement. "Are you talking about the original Skyway Bridge collapse?" he asked.

"Yes."

He had been on a family vacation in Texas at the time but how could he forget the headlines—*Freighter strikes bridge during driving squall...collapses southbound span...spills bus and passenger cars into the bay...thirty-some people killed.*

"Yes, I remember it, but what does it have to do with Charlene's sister?"

Morgan tapped loose several more jellybeans, leaned back in his chair, and again flung them in the direction of his mouth, this time all of them hitting their mark. "Want some?" he asked.

"No thanks, I just had breakfast," Adam said, anxious for the guy to continue his account.

"Charlene's sister was one of the victims who was dumped into the bay and killed," Morgan said straight out.

Adam's mind churned at the news. "Was she alone?"

Morgan clasped his hands behind his head. "Apparently, she was traveling alone on the bus that went over. Pardon the pun, but now you know why I'm surprised Charlene's death did not make a bigger splash down your way."

"Right," he said, still attempting to put the news in perspective.

"I'll tell you another thing I learned in doing a little research on the story I will be doing for the paper this week. The day Charlene jumped to her death...May ninth? It's the same day the original bridge collapsed seven years earlier."

It's where I belong.

"Obviously, a connection," he lamely replied.

"Obvious to me and you," Morgan said. "You can be sure it will be mentioned in my story."

"Anything else you found worthy of note?" he asked, sounding like a reporter himself.

"Only the who, what, when, and where. The *why* I'm leaving to the shrinks. It's a suicide, after all," he said, underscoring Peterson's observation about the media's approach to the matter. "Like I said, I didn't know Charlene personally. If you're looking for info along those lines, you might want to talk to her pastor over in Hidden Valley. His name is Gordon Conroy of the First Baptist Church. He was the man who buried her."

"Buried where?"

"In a little cemetery adjacent to the church—operated by it, as a matter of fact. You may have driven right by the place on the way over."

"Yes, I did," he said, recalling the olive-colored structure with the steeple, sitting all alone on the outskirts of town.

"Would you like for me to give the reverend a ring to see if he's in—let him know you will be dropping by?" Morgan pushed his frame up from the desk. "His office is right inside the church."

"No, no need for that. I'm going by his way, anyhow," Adam said, rising to give Morgan a parting handshake.

*

The question of why hung with him in the truck like a keepsake on a rearview mirror. A woman leaps to her death at the same spot where her sister lost her own life in a tragic accident seven years earlier. What would the mental health people make of it? Cite it as a prime example of sibling inseparability? Was it reason enough for the sister to say it's where she belonged? Better yet, is this where *he* belonged?

Adam swung into the church's parking lot, noting the cemetery sitting on a gentle rise of land to the building's rear. He drove past a brick bulletin board bordered by well-kept gladiolus beds, pulling to a stop next to a late model silver sedan parked near the side entrance that he took to be the pastor's. He knocked twice and was about to knock a third time when the door opened. There to greet him was an elderly, distinguished looking man dressed in a dark blue suit and yellow tie.

"Pastor Conroy?" he asked, wondering if "Reverend" would have been more proper.

"Yes," he said. "How can I help you?"

"My name is Adam Fraley. Frank Morgan, editor of the *Weekly Courier*, referred me to you. He said you may be able to provide me some information on a woman by the name of Charlene Gibbs."

The pastor eyed him for an instant. "Are you a reporter?"

"No, just an acquaintance of Charlene."

"Oh...okay," he said in a resigned manner, leaving Adam the feeling if it hadn't been a church door he was standing in front of, he may not have been receiving a gesture to step inside.

As it was, he entered an office as ordered as Frank Morgan's was disordered. It was furnished with what appeared to be antique pieces, the kind he was terrified to sit on for fear of crumbling them, despite his average build.

The pastor pointed him to a side chair positioned next to his roll-top desk.

"So Mr. Morgan said you should speak to me about Charlene Gibbs," he said, carefully lowering his frail body into the desk chair. "You say you are an acquaintance of hers?"

"Yes, from Tampa, and I appreciate you taking the time to speak with me."

"Well, it's such a sad, sad story. I'm not sure I fully understand it," he said, folding his hands in his lap. "Is there anything in particular you would like to know?"

"I thought you might have some insight into what could have driven her over the edge."

He furrowed his brow and slowly shook his head. "I don't know. She had such a happy childhood. Jake and Arlene Gibbs were wonderful, hardworking, God-fearing parents—small dairy farmers in case you didn't know."

Watching and listening to the pastor, Adam couldn't help but imagine the profile he might once have projected at the pulpit—sagging shoulders a bit more rounded—thin gray hair a shade darker—rich voice a mite stronger—and blue eyes a bit brighter.

"...the girls gave them no trouble."

"What was her sister's name?"

The pastor's mouth curved into a smile. "Carlene. It was Arlene, Carlene, and Charlene. Jake always was joking he had Colleen in reserve. He preferred it to Darlene, though I think he would have liked a Jack or Jerry to come along to start evening things out."

"Was Carlene an older sister?"

"Yes, by about five years."

"They must have been very close from the way you describe the family."

He nodded before shifting to a more comfortable position in his chair.

"I don't want to make it sound like the family didn't go through some rough periods. After all, they were small farmers and at times scratched out a living. During one particularly severe down year, they even took the step of converting a storehouse on the property into a small bed and breakfast unit to supplement their income."

"Did it work out okay?"

"They did quite well by it. Fishermen, especially, found it a convenient overnight accommodation. As a matter of fact, you could say the bed and breakfast idea is what led to Carlene getting married."

"How so?" he asked, nudging the pastor along.

"Jake told me early on about this one father and son fishing team who stayed there quite often. He said the son seemed to be taking a liking to Carlene who was a senior in high school around the time."

"He was worried about it?"

The pastor leaned back in his chair and narrowed his eyes, as though giving it some thought. "No, not worried. He said the father was from a well-to-do Indiana family. Anyway, as the story goes, Carlene graduated and ended up going to Ohio College, which is not far from here. And who do you think was already enrolled there as a student?"

"The son of course—did they have it all planned beforehand?"

"Maybe or maybe not. I posed the same question to Jake and Arlene. They were not sure. As it turned out, the two continued their relationship in college and ended up getting married with their parents' blessing."

"They were married here?"

"Yes, in this very church, and by me. It was a small ceremony, attended mainly by family members and a few friends."

"And they ended up in Tampa."

"Yes, and that's when I began to lose touch with her."

"Do you recall what year it was?"

"Well…let me think," he said, raising his finger to his lips. "Oh, sometime in the late seventies, I'd say. I could look it up if you like."

"No, that's okay. What was her husband's name?"

The pastor widened his eyes, again pressing his memory. "Wheeler was the last name. Monte, I believe, was the first. Yes…Monte Wheeler."

"Did they have children?"

"No, and perhaps it was a blessing, considering what happened later. The tragedies befalling that family…it's a shame."

"The parents were alive when Carlene was killed?"

"Yes, they died one right after the other in 1982, the mother from cancer, the father from a heart attack."

"Where was Charlene when her sister was killed?"

He tilted his head to the side in wonderment. "I'm surprised you don't know. She also was living in Tampa."

"I didn't meet her until after her sister's death," he immediately said.

"Yes, Charlene moved to Tampa after she graduated from high school. You know how it goes with kids from small towns. They want to head for the big city as soon as the high school diploma is in hand. Her parents would have preferred she attend college, but Charlene did not possess the intellectual curiosity of her sister. Moreover, Carlene was urging her to come to Florida, letting her know how exciting the life was down there and promising the parents she would look out for her. Unfortunately, it was Carlene who needed looking after.

"In what way?"

The pastor took a deep breath before answering, as if reluctant to continue much longer with the personal insight. "She called home one day to tell her parents she had been diagnosed with Hodgkin's lymphoma and would be starting treatments soon."

"Tough news for someone her age."

"Apparently, it is a form of cancer that can strike at a young age."

"I assume she beat it?"

"Eventually, it appeared so, but from what her parents said, she went through a rough period with the chemo and radiation treatments."

"The diagnosis occurred after Charlene's move to Tampa?"

"Yes, and it eased the parents' concern somewhat knowing her sister was nearby to help in her recovery."

"Did they visit her?"

"Yes, on a couple of occasions they went down for a visit."

"At the time of the bridge collapse, what was her state?"

"By that time she was considered in a state of remission and getting back on her feet."

"Well enough to travel?"

"Yes, well enough to make it up here for a Christmas visit."

"And it all changed when the ship hit the Skyway," he said.

"What about later on, did—"

"Tell me, Mr. Fraley, how long did you say you knew Charlene?" the pastor interjected, undoubtedly puzzled why he was having to provide the details to Charlene's life to someone who claimed to be an acquaintance of hers.

"Not long enough, I'm afraid."

"Do you mind if I ask...were you a sweetheart of hers?"

"Oh no...no, more of a confidant at the end, I'd say."

The pastor eyed him as though he was ready with a follow-up question but then hesitated. "Would you like to go see the family's gravesite?" he asked.

"Yes, I would."

He followed him out the door and up a curved stepping-stone path leading to a wrought iron fence surrounding well-manicured grounds, its grass cover cut precisely to the edges of the markers.

"A volunteer group at our church has overall responsibility for cemetery operations," he said, swinging open the gate. "We get our share of graffiti but no major vandalism to speak of."

He trailed the pastor past a succession of gravestones, a few tilting from age, but most standing tall, to the Gibbs family plot located in a far corner of the property. Three white marble markers, each simply inscribed with the deceased's name and position in the family, stood side by side. They stopped before the one with the freshly turned earth. Charlene Gibbs...Daughter...Born January 9, 1962...Died May 9, 1987.

Minutes passed in silence as they stood at the foot of the gravesite and reflected on the mystery of it all. If only he had been quicker off the mark, Adam thought, grabbed her in time, they wouldn't be standing here listening to the wind moaning in the trees. He lifted his eyes. Overhead, the limbs of nearby elms crooked skyward, their leaves flitting in the bright sunlight. Charlene had found her peace. It was up to him to find his.

"Look there," the pastor said, breaking the spell.

He followed his outstretched hand directed at two nearby

gravesites. Carved into the headstones were the names Josephine Fraley and Felix Fraley.

"Any relation to you?" he asked through a smile.

"Not that I know of," he replied. "I once planned a genealogy search on the name at the suggestion of my parents but never got around to it. I do recall having a great uncle living in Ohio, however."

"Can't say I know much concerning the Fraley Family. They were here long before I arrived," he said, shaking his head. "Why don't we take a look at the ledger back at the church? It may give us a clue as to where they were from."

"There are people from out of the region buried here?" he asked on the walk back.

"Oh, yes. People move to warmer climates or to be near their children but end up wishing to be buried in their home town."

The pastor retrieved from a bottom desk drawer an embossed purple ledger and started to leaf through it, a faint tremor visible in his hands.

"It's in alphabetical order," he said, laying the ledger open on the desk and sliding his forefinger down columns of handwritten entries.

"Beautiful handwriting," Adam commented from over the pastor's shoulder.

"My wife serves as the sexton, so to speak. She is a perfectionist and even took a course in calligraphy to prepare for the job. Here we are...the F's," he said, stopping his finger on the Fraley name. "See, it says in the far right column...purchased in 1939 by Josephine Fraley of Mobile, Alabama."

"Yes, I see," Adam said, though his attention already had moved to the G's on the same page and the Gibbs entry where it was noted two plots were purchased by a Charlene Gibbs of Hidden Valley in June of 1985."

"Do you have kin in Alabama?" the pastor asked.

"None I know of," he replied.

The pastor closed the ledger. "There's something else you might like to see," he said eagerly, picking through another desk drawer to draw out a folder. "Our volunteer group has an ongoing project to compile family photographs of church members to keep on file."

The pastor pinched a large colored photograph from the folder and laid it on the desk, nudging it toward him for a better view.

"I told you Carlene made it up here for a Christmas visit. This was taken in the Gibbs living room right after the New Year's holiday in 1980. You can see in the background the Christmas tree is still up," he said, working his wavering finger across the photograph. "Here you can see through the living room window...."

All he was seeing, he would have liked to have told the reverend, was a stunning set of clear violet eyes, wide and alive, peering from an otherwise familiar face, the missing piece of an indelible image framed by the events of a midnight hour.

"...the outline of the storehouse they converted."

"I also notice here an antique wall clock," he said, pointing to the background of the photo. "It looks a lot like the one Charlene kept in her apartment."

The reverend shifted his view and nodded his head. "Same one. She loved that clock. Her parents gave it to her as a going-away present when she left for Florida, a memento of her childhood here."

"I understand the disposal of her personal possessions was handled by an in-law."

"Yes. I inquired about it and was informed by the local sheriff her brother-in-law would see to it they were disposed of properly. She did not take much with her at all and certainly wasn't there long enough to accumulate much."

"Backing up a moment. How long was it after her sister's death that Charlene returned to Hidden Valley?" he asked.

The pastor looked to the ceiling, collecting his thoughts. "It would have been sometime in 1981, I believe, not long before her parents passed away. It was her wish to be with them during their final days."

"I know this may be an inappropriate request, Pastor Conroy, but is there any chance you have an extra print of this photo you could spare? I do not have a single photo of Charlene and would like to have this one to take with me."

He thought for a second. "I don't see why not," he said, handing the photo to him. "I have the negative in the folder here. I'll have one of the volunteers get another print made for the file."

"Thank you, though I feel I owe you a payment of some kind."

"No, no payment," he said, waving a dismissive hand. "I tell you what...the next time you are in a church make a little donation on my behalf," he said with a twinkle in his eye.

"Will do."

The pastor glanced at his watch and exhaled a deep breath. "Well now, Mr. Fraley, in a few minutes I must go meet my wife for lunch. I'm afraid I'll have to close this conversation."

Adam would have liked to have plied him for more, delved into the details of Charlene's life in Hidden Valley following her return, but realized he would have to settle for what he had. Therefore, with photo in hand, he headed for the door, pausing and turning for one final question. "Pastor Conroy...looking at this picture and listening to what you said about the closeness of the Gibbs family, did anyone ever consider having Carlene buried next to her parents in the family plot or having her body transferred here?"

"No," he said, crinkling his brow to show his puzzlement at the question.

*

Adam stopped by Molly's Kitchen for lunch on the way back, unable to bypass the $4.95 chicken-fried steak special with choice of dessert bannered on the chalkboard. Seven hours later he was exiting the interstate at Strawberry Hills for one of his frequent unannounced visits to his parents.

When he joined the Air Force to see the world and ended up stationed an hour away from home, he suspected it was not only a laugh-or-cry moment for him but also for his folks. For twenty-five years his father operated a small fleet of produce-hauling trucks. While his mother kept the books straight Adam helped keep the trucks clean as his rite of passage. Following high school he hung around for a couple of years to lend a helping hand to his parents during the difficult economic downturn of the seventies. Runaway inflation was eating into profits, threatening to sink the operation. About to go under, the family caught a break when a speculator made an offer to buy the company in anticipation of an economic recovery. The sale, along with their social security benefits, provided his parents enough to retire on. Prior to the downturn he considered the option of one day taking over the business. But as his father advised, the competition from the large trucking firms loomed large and likely would drive him out of business, the same as they did the small farms, so he probably would be better off in the long haul learning a trade. On the heels of the sale, he decided to do so with the help of the Air Force.

In retrospect, he came to realize his visits home were a way of keeping himself grounded in the common sense of his parents' household. They had managed to get him through the teenage years and eventually out of the house in one piece and as their reward, his father wryly observed, watched him reappear with all the regularity of a homesick Swallow. From his point of view it sure beat any kind of military R & R.

Perhaps it was a premonition on his mother's part but once he left for the service, she saw to it his upstairs room was kept intact. On his returns he would set aside time to lay in his old bed and gaze out a wall of windows to a stand of trees bordering the family's gray, clapboard home built against the back of a hill. It was the way it always was and through the years gave him the feeling of growing up in a tree house. "Maybe we should get you a rope ladder," his father once quipped.

Saturday evening over dinner he filled them in on his new job, his mother expressing concern for his safety, his father over his commitment to school. He reassured them on both accounts mindful he forever would be a child in their eyes.

Halfway through dinner, however, came the question Adam half expected.

"Any word yet on your discharge appeal?" his father asked.

"Not yet," he said. "It should be coming down soon."

"Makes quite a difference, I understand, having a general discharge on your record rather than an honorable one."

"No question," came Adam's curt reply.

"Julie Waterman asked about you," his mother said, coming to his rescue.

"Julie Waterman may have been the other reason he joined the military," his father said, taking up the topic.

Unfortunately, there was an element of truth to his father's remark. Julie Waterman would have made a wonderful wife—to someone else, he would come to discover nearly too late.

They were high school sweethearts, having been pegged so by peers following back-to-back dates to the senior prom and the town's Strawberry Festival Parade. From that point on, expectations among students, parents, and townspeople became the glue to keep the relationship intact through the remainder of school and thereafter, right up until he took off for the service.

As he explained to his parents, by most measures of goodness, Julie was a far better person than he. It was simply that she did not share his adventuresome spirit. Asked by his mother to elaborate, he said he wasn't sure he could without sounding like he was putting her down in some way.

Fortunately, Julie came to understand, accepting his tortured explanations shortly before he set out to follow his misbegotten dream of traveling the world.

"Tell her hello for me," he said to his mother, ending the after-dinner conversation.

The next day they resurrected a ritual from Sunday afternoons past and dug out the family's hand-crank ice cream maker to churn out a batch of his favorite flavor—maple nut. Few culinary experiences could trigger a memory in him like the taste of homemade ice cream. He recalled the fun parts from years past…the trip to a neighbor's backyard ice house, set up for sport and commercial fishermen, to pick up the blocks of ice, the loading of them into burlap sacks, the lugging of the sacks home, the splintering of the blocks with an ice pick, the stuffing of the ice and the rock salt into the wooden bucket surrounding the metal can holding the ice cream mixture, the turning of the hand crank, the intermittent removal of the container to check the texture of the mixture, the emptying and the eating. In the end, he could never decide which was the more enjoyable, the making or the tasting.

Sunday evening he was back on the road for the last leg of his trip, his stomach settled, his mind back on the bridge.

CHAPTER FOUR

First thing Monday morning, Peterson's wife was on the phone letting Adam know her husband would not be able to make it into work because of flight delays. Not to worry, she said, he would be there in the morning—a message he subsequently passed along to the two prospective clients his boss had noted on his calendar to see. And worry, he wouldn't. If he learned anything in the Air Force, it was how to keep a facility safe and secure during downtime, no matter how small the operation. "When it comes to your duties and responsibilities think in terms of places, not people," a sergeant of his famously said on one of their regular patrols of base installations, perhaps subscribing to the neutron bomb theory of warfare.

For the remainder of the workday, he alternately checked the computer files, answered the phone, and chatted with walk-ins, half of whom were looking for directions, until it was time to close shop. He then made a beeline for the downtown public library. In a first-floor corner alcove he found what he was looking for—a row of shelves stacked with city directories dating back several decades. He set up shop at an adjacent empty table. An invaluable resource for people finders, the city directories were a mother lode of information compared to the phone books. Along with phone numbers and addresses, there were spouse's names and workplaces to be found. He started with the 1985 edition and worked his way back year-by-year until he found a listing for a Charlene Gibbs in the 1981 volume. To his surprise and probably to her former neighbor Rosemary's, if she had been made aware, Charlene was shown to be living at the same Mid-Town apartments. Her place of employment was listed as the La Veranda restaurant. An identical entry showed up again in the 1980 directory before disappearing from the books in the prior year. Next, he checked for the name Monte Wheeler in the 1980 directory and found one with a wife named Carlene. It was his place of employment, however, that grabbed Adam's attention, for Monte Wheeler, husband of Carlene, was listed as City Editor for the Bay Area Beacon.

His next stop was the library's microfilm room where he pulled up the May 8, 1980 edition of the Beacon. As expected the stories related to the bridge collapse were splashed across the front page. In scrolling through them he noted a box with bold black borders halfway down the page containing a brief note.

The Beacon staff wishes to express its deepest sympathy to the family of Monte Wheeler, the Beacon's City Editor, whose wife was one of those tragically killed in the collapse of the Skyway Bridge.

Adam rewound the reel and placed it in a return tray on top of an adjacent file cabinet. From there he walked to the library's periodical reading room and searched through a stack of 1980 regional magazines, flipping through endless pages of wedding pictures, engagement announcements, and civic club activities. In an April issue of one called the Bay View, he came across a photo of Carlene Wheeler being presented an award by the Estuary Preservation Society—in the background stood her husband. He next pulled the current day's issue of the *Beacon* from the reading rack. He flipped through the pages until he lighted on the masthead. There, at the top, was the name Monte Wheeler, listed as the paper's Executive Editor.

The guy's been riding a very fast career track, he said to himself.

*

La Veranda restaurant was at the least three or four stars up from Adam's usual dining out experience. Once a turn-of-the-century home located only a stone's throw from the downtown waterfront, it was converted into an eating establishment by a couple of enterprising Cuban immigrants. Shaded by a giant overhanging banyan tree, its mix of tranquil pastel colors, cozy rooms, historic wall photos, wrap-around porch, wrought iron balconies, and outdoor gardens offered local movers and shakers an ideal informal gathering spot to compare notes. Fortunately, he arrived late for the lunchtime crowd and sat alone at the empty bar munching a side order of potato skins. Working through the appetizer, he watched a blond-haired bartender, outfitted in a starched white shirt, black pants and bow tie, wash glasses with the fervor of a man ready to end his shift.

"Say, do you by chance remember a gal by the name of Charlene Gibbs who worked here some years back?" he asked.

"Nope," the bartender answered, reaching for a towel to dry his hands. "I've only been at this job for a year."

"Anyone else around who might recall her?" Adam asked, aware he was sending the message it wasn't the potato skins he was there for.

"How long ago are we talking about?" he asked.

"Seven…eight years."

"The only guy I know who's been around for that long is Steve Brand, the manager, and he's not here today."

"You know where I might find him?" he asked, crunching down on the last of the skins.

The barkeep turned around to take a glance at a wall clock. "Right about now I'd say he's probably over at the Town Center Tennis Club hitting a few. From what I'm told, that's where he spends most of his days off," he said, exchanging the bar tab for Adam's empty dish.

"Private club?"

"No, it's public—run by the city. I've played there once or twice."

"Where's it located?" he prodded, dropping a generous tip on the counter.

"Over near Westside Park not far from here. You can see it from the street. Look for the tall fences with the green canvas windscreens. They surround the place. You can't miss it."

And he didn't, pulling his pickup into a parking lot to the rear of the complex. Finding it nearly empty led him to believe the club's members were blessed with an abundance of common sense, opting to take their swings in the cool of the morning or evening rather than on an asphalt surface baked by a brutal midday sun.

He entered a tiny clubhouse to observe a red-haired girl of college age, dressed in pink shorts and tank top, sitting on a bar stool behind the service counter with legs crossed, elbow on knee, chin in hand, and freckled face buried in a paperback

"Good afternoon," he said, scrambling her from her perch.

Setting aside the paperback, she looked at him expectantly. "Can I help you?"

"Yes, you can. I'm here to meet a man by the name of Steve Brand. I was told I could find him here around this time of day."

She looked out a large window to the cluster of courts, only one of which was occupied. She then glanced down to a logbook, placing a finger under a name.

"Mr. Brand is one of the men in the foursome out there," she said.

"Can you tell me for how long they have the court scheduled?"

She looked down at the log. "Another half hour."

"If you don't mind, I'll wait for him at the table over there," he said, motioning toward a corner snack bar. "When he finishes could you let him know I'm waiting to see him?"

"Sure," she said with a fleeting look of curiosity, before returning to her stool and paperback.

He sprung a can of orange juice loose from a vending machine and took a seat facing the courts. For a few minutes he watched the four go at each other in a style more befitting a game of badminton, patting balls toward whatever corner of the court was empty at the moment.

No sense trying to figure out which one was Brand, he concluded, reaching into his briefcase to retrieve his Shakespeare textbook so he could catch up on a class assignment.

He was well into it, reading about Prospero's innocent daughter Miranda getting all worked up over seeing a young man for the first time in her life, when the tennis foursome came bounding into the clubhouse.

They gathered at the counter to chat for some time with the redhead. For a moment Adam doubted whether she was going to relay his message, till one of the men jerked his head in his direction. Several handshakes and parting jibes later, a barrel-chested man with matted gray hair sprouting from a head the size of a watermelon broke from the pack and headed his way, swabbing his flushed face with one hand while lugging his tennis bag with the other.

"I'm told you're waiting to see me?" he said in a husky voice.

Adam rose to greet him. "Yes, Mr. Brand. My name is Adam Fraley. A member of the staff over at the La Veranda referred me to you," he said, wasting no time in playing his calling card.

"Oh, is that right?" he said, relaxing a bit.

They shook hands and took seats, Brand dipping into his bag to exchange his towel for an oversized water bottle.

"What brings you here?"

"A family mission, sort of. I understand you once had a young woman by the name of Charlene Gibbs working for you—am I right?"

"Charlene Gibbs," he repeated, drawing the name out. "Sure, I remember her. Worked as a hostess for maybe a year and a half. Why do you ask?"

Brand alternated between taking gulps of air and water in an attempt to recover from his bout with the heat.

"Perhaps you haven't heard, but Charlene died a short while back from a suicide."

Brand stopped in mid-gulp. "My God," he said, lowering the bottle. "Sorry to hear that. Is this what you came to tell me?"

"It's only part of the reason. My primary mission is on behalf of the family. As part of their remembrance of her, we have decided to compile a family history."

"A genealogy?"

"No, more like a family narrative that will include brief profiles. We thought it might help those she left behind to come to terms with her suicide, maybe even prevent others under similar duress from following the same course. We're thinking of distributing it to crisis centers and other social agencies."

"I don't know whether I will be able to contribute much," Brand said, indifferent to the idea. "I only knew her in a professional capacity."

"Of course, we assumed as much, but still thought you might be able to give us whatever information you can relating to her job. Since her life was cut short, we are searching for anything of a worthwhile substance to include."

Brand shrugged his shoulders and wiped his mouth with the back of his hand.

"Charlene was everything you could ask for in a hostess: polite, pleasant, dependable–just a very good worker."

"Straight-laced, from what I understand," Adam said.

"Yes, very much so. She was a simple small-town girl with small-town values. I once was told by another waitress of mine that some guy from one of the gentleman's clubs was trying like hell to convince her to come on board with them, but she would have none of it," he said, his breathing returning to normal. "Other than that, I don't know if there is much I can tell you."

"Her first job on settling here was with you?" Adam asked, pushing the conversation.

"I believe it was. If I recall right, it was her first job out of high school."

"She had a sister named Carlene. Did she ever mention her or other members of the family?"

"She didn't talk family much, but yes, I did meet her sister."

"How so?"

"Charlene brought her over one evening to introduce me to her. She had just arrived with her husband for dinner."

"Monte Wheeler?"

"Yes. You know him?"

"Indirectly. Isn't he one of the influential types I hear frequents La Veranda?"

"Yes," Brand replied, leaving it at that.

"What about his relationship with Charlene? Anything there of note?"

Brand tossed his empty water bottle into a corner trash can, as he considered the question. "They were in-laws. What else is there to say?"

"She worked there. He frequented there. I thought you might have noticed a special family bond on display between the two, something I could highlight. No?" Adam asked, pushing more.

"Not sure what you're driving at," Brand said, obviously annoyed at the line of questioning.

"How did she handle the news of her sister getting killed in the Skyway Bridge collapse?" he asked, deciding on a different direction.

"How do you think? It came as a shock to all of us."

"Was she scheduled to work the day the bridge collapsed?"

"No. She had the day off, thank God," he said. "I for one wouldn't have wanted to be around when she got the news."

"Do you have any idea where her sister was headed on the bus?"

"Charlene mentioned later on she was on her way to Miami to visit in-laws. Apparently, she had some qualms about flying."

"What eventually became of Charlene?"

"She quit a few weeks after her sister's death. Gave no reason other than to say she was planning a different direction in her life. It was the last I saw or heard of her until you came along."

"And Wheeler?"

"Are you planning on interviewing him also?" he asked, a note of anxiety creeping into his voice.

"Not sure, but what became of him after his wife's death?"

"A few months later he started showing up again for lunch. A year or so later, he showed up with a new wife. Introduced her around to everyone."

"To you?"

"Me also...he knows how not to wait in line for a table," Brand said, smiling thinly.

"Who was she?"

"Ward Fletcher's niece."

"And who's Ward Fletcher?" Adam asked, as though he didn't know.

"Are you from here or Ohio?"

"Here."

"The sheriff. Don't you ever read the paper?"

*

"You seem disappointed," Peterson remarked in reaction to Adam's accounts of his trip and his talk with Brand.

He reached into his briefcase, pulled out the Gibbs family photo the pastor provided him, and slid it across the desk to his boss who held it to the light.

"Why, it will probably take me at least an hour to figure out which one is Charlene," he said, giving Adam a deadpanned look before handing it back.

"Unfortunately, the trip did go a long way in explaining why she felt she belonged there, though I'm sure there's more to the story."

"It's a very old story, Adam. A pretty girl from a small town moves to the big city and immediately men start trying to take her clothes off through one means or the other."

"That's boiling life down to the basics," Adam said.

"It's another thing I've learned in this business. Beauty can be a curse as well as a blessing to a woman— depends on one's perspective. Women like to be desired and men like to possess. The problem is this damn little thing called civilization keeps getting in the way, creating all sorts of stumbling blocks."

"Maybe it's more of a case of who's got the power."

"Hey, don't automatically take up the female's side," Peterson said. "Beauty may have a relatively short lifespan but, when in play, it often overpowers anything the male of the species can come up with."

"I took the photo over to the Mid-Town Apartments to show it to Rosemary, the old woman I was talking to the other day. She wasn't sure if the guy she saw visiting Charlene was the same man in the photo," he said. "Understandable, considering her age and the fact he was seven years younger at the time."

"Was that Wheeler in the photo?" Peterson asked with interest. "Let me take another look at it."

He passed the photo to his boss for a second look.

"That's him standing next to the older fellow?"

"Yes…behind Charlene's sister."

"Not a bad-looking guy."

Peterson handed the photo back, snatched a copy of the morning paper lying on the desk, and began leafing through the pages until he came to the one with the masthead printed on it, at which point he placed a finger on a name.

"Monte Wheeler, Executive Editor," Peterson said. "Would never had known it, if you hadn't brought it to my attention."

"Don't feel alone," he said. "How many people are there who bother to look at the masthead?"

"Yeah, they think the whole thing is passed down from Mount Olive," Peterson said in disgust.

"Mount Sinai you mean."

"Mount Sinai…whatever."

"How do you suppose she got on the bridge, Pete?"

"Could have walked—highly unlikely—too far and not allowed on the bridge. Could have driven—unlikely, since she had no car and none was found abandoned. Could have taken a taxi—unlikely, given her state of mind. Could have hitched a ride—unlikely, out of character for her. Could have been driven there by someone she knew—likely."

"Is it possible to gain access to those closed-circuit tapes?"

"You want to see yourself in action?"

"I want to see all the parties involved in the action if possible. But it would mean reviewing the tapes and I'm not so sure the government would allow access to the evidence."

"What the hell do you mean—the evidence? You say it as if a crime has been committed. As it stands now, it is not even classified as an accident. It's a suicide, plain and simple."

"So you think a viewing is possible?"

"There's been a lot of static raised recently about allowing the public access to government security tapes. As far as I know, they're still a matter of public record. I tell you what, I'll get old Victor Gantt, the insurance guy down the hall, to give us a hand. I've done enough workmen's comp snooping on the side for him to warrant a favor. I'm sure he can come up with some cockeyed story about Charlene having had a life insurance policy and how he as the insurance investigator needs access to the tapes to verify that it was in fact a suicide."

The desk phone buzzed, prompting Peterson to reach over and punch the hold button.

"Do you think we should call first? Let them know we will be coming?"

"No. Why give them advance notice? Just make like it's routine business. Chances are it will be some low-level clerk minding the storeroom. Victor can wiggle his way into anything."

"And on the outside chance I will be recognized?"

The phone again buzzed and Peterson punched a second caller on hold.

"A very outside chance. And if you are, Victor can claim he wanted the key witness to be there with him."

He noticed the first of the blinking lights on the phone disappear.

"You said Wheeler married the sheriff's niece?"

"It's what Brand said—yes. Do you know her?"

"Don't know her. Know him a bit. Can't say anything really good or bad about him. He has a reputation of being from the kick-butt school and a stickler for the rules."

He noticed the second of the hold lights on the phone go out.

"Look, Pete, I know this is taking up company time. Like you've said, we don't do pro bono work."

His boss nodded in agreement. "That's true, but I have to confess, the case intrigues me. I'm not a journalist, but you're right, it should have been more of a story."

The phone buzzed and this time his boss grabbed the receiver. "Peterson," he snapped. "Oh, Mrs. Gordon, yes, I have your report. Can you meet me at my place this afternoon at three? Good. See you then."

"I forgot to ask. How did the Belize trip work out?"

"Not like she expected it would," Peterson said, drawing a folder from his briefcase. "Here's a copy of my surveillance report you can enter into the records."

"Do I have to read it to get the verdict?" he asked, taking it in hand.

"The verdict in this instance is not guilty. It comes after a complete weekend of boredom, mainly hanging around a hotel lobby and piano bar and putt-putting around a golf course full of too many hazards for hours on end."

"He never left the hotel area?"

"Once," he said. "I thought at the time this might be what Mrs. Gordon had in mind in sending me down there."

Peterson leaned back in his chair and folded his hands behind his head. "Saturday evening he took off on foot from the hotel. I followed him from a safe distance as he hoofed it down several blocks of residential streets. 'Oh, here we go,' I said to myself. He has a Latin honey on the side and he is about to rendezvous with her—probably at her place. Well, it turns out my suspicions were about as accurate as Mrs. Gordon's. After trailing him for another block or two, I see some increase in sidewalk foot traffic—people looking like they were congregating for some neighborhood event, maybe one of those South American street festivals, with Gordon now among them. Next thing you know, I was part of a congregation, sitting in this little Catholic church doing the stand-up, sit-down, kneel-down routine a few pews behind him."

"He was headed for church and lured a lost soul there," Adam chuckled to his boss.

"Yeah, it's a wonder the thunder and lightning didn't start up the moment I entered."

"Did you drop anything into the collection box?"

"I only had a Hamilton on me and I wasn't about to drop it in the can, so I passed. The guy sitting next to me looked like he was going to take out a machete, lop my head off, and drop it into the box," he said. "But hey, you got to do what you got to do."

"You can't chalk up a donation as a travel expense?"

"Not in my outfit," he said, grabbing his water bottle for a mouthful.

"Say, Pete, there's one other item from my trip I wanted to run by you."

"What's that?"

"The pastor's wife keeps a ledger on the cemetery operation.

Next to the entry for the Gibbs family, she noted the purchase of two plots by Charlene."

"So?"

"So, she purchased them after her parents' deaths."

"Was she planning on moving her sister up there?"

"I asked the pastor the same question when I was leaving and he said no."

"Well then, what did he give for a reason?"

"I didn't ask. He was unaware I saw his wife's notation in the record and before I could get around to pressing him on it, he cut the conversation off, saying he had a meeting to make."

Peterson adopted a contemplative look, slowly rotating his water bottle on the desk with his thumb and forefinger.

"Her sister is dead. Her parents are dead. She had no other family to speak of and no close female friends, from what you tell me, right?"

"Right."

"And your question is who is the *she* in the I-hope-she-understands comment she made on the bridge and my answer is I don't know, though I'm thinking you're thinking the same thing I'm thinking."

*

Victor Gantt was less the gatecrasher than Peterson portrayed him to be. When briefed on the Gibbs case over the phone, the insurance man recommended an advance call by his firm's in-house lawyer, if they expected him to participate. It turned out to be a wise strategy, as the lawyer learned the tapes considered evidential were stored separately in a secured cabinet, while the remaining tapes were kept for a period of less than thirty days before being purged. The tapes covering the interval when the jumping incident occurred were not being held as evidence, since they were not part of a criminal investigation, the lawyer explained. The path thus paved, he and Gantt, a sandy-haired man with drawn face and a lanky build, trooped to the Department of

Transportation where a clerk with the personality to match the sterile cast of the room greeted them.

"You'll need to sign for them," the clerk said, settling for Gantt's signature alone.

"You want the entire day's worth?" he asked.

"How about we start with three hours' worth…ten in the evening to one in the morning," Gantt replied.

The clerk sauntered back to a cabinet and a minute later returned with a stack of tapes on a cart.

"You're fortunate in asking for these now. They're scheduled for erasing in three days' time," he said. He then pointed to the rear of the room. "You can use the VCR and monitor mounted on the video stand in the back. I hope you brought a boatload of patience with you. People don't realize how long it takes to sit and go through them," he added. "If you're trying to find something on the woman who took the leap, I can tell you there's nothing there. The sheriff's people have already gone through them."

"Is that right?" Gantt said in feigned surprise.

"You need to keep in mind the cameras are there to monitor the bridge, not the people on it," the clerk said to their backs in a last bit of advice, as they strode past head-high tiers of cabinets to the rear of the room, out of earshot of the guy.

A preliminary spot check of the tapes underscored what the clerk pointed out. Narrow in range and scope, they were not the normal output of true surveillance cameras. At best they provided snippets of traffic flows on and off the bridge and activity around the toll plazas. Overhead views of northbound and southbound lanes came by way of cameras mounted above, while sections of bridge railing popped in and out of view from cameras mounted at road level. As it was, a careful screening of the limited sectional shots of the northbound lane and railing turned up nothing other than a glimpse of Adam's truck briefly popping in and out of view, so they decided to concentrate on activity at the northbound toll plaza.

"Why don't we fast-forward ahead to see if we can pick up the emergency vehicles arriving," he suggested to Gantt who was busy punching buttons from a folding chair positioned next to the stand. "We can then work back an hour. It could save us some time."

Gantt pressed the fast-forward button, intermittently stopping the tape to check the time recorder at the bottom of the screen. At half past midnight, the first of the flashing lights of law enforcement units rolled into view at the northbound toll plaza.

"How far do you want me to back this thing up?" Gantt asked.

"Let's go back an hour and a half to around eleven," Adam replied.

"What makes you think we're going to spot something the sheriff's people didn't?" he asked, rewinding the tape.

"It's nothing more than a second opinion we are formulating," Adam responded, tapping his notepad with the back of his pen. "By the way, Pete tells me nobody knows their makes of cars better than you."

"I also do auto insurance claims. It's my business to know cars. Why?" he asked, lifting his glasses from his nose to rub his steel gray eyes.

"I'd appreciate it if you could keep an eye on the toll plaza and scribble down every make of car passing through it, till you see my pickup. You can skip the obvious: buses, large trucks, government vehicles. Can you do that?"

"For an hour's time?"

"Yes, and while you're monitoring the cars, I'll keep an eye out for people."

"Cars look a lot alike nowadays. I won't be able to be exact on all of them but I'll give it a try. It's a damn good thing we're not looking at rush-hour traffic or we'd soon be looking cross-eyed," he said, leaning over to punch the play button.

As Gantt scribbled Adam kept watch on drivers and passengers. Clear shots of faces, however, unlike all the extended arms, were few and far between. Still, he was convinced Charlene and a companion were sitting in one of those cars, and neither in a pleasant frame of mind.

An hour later his pickup crawled into view, signaling the final act of the drama and the end of their search.

"Now I need to find out what make of car Wheeler drives," he said to Gantt, rewinding the tape.

"No problem, I can get that easy enough," the insurance man said, removing his glasses. "I'll have it to you in the morning."

"All finished?" the clerk asked, as they returned the tapes.

"For now," Gantt said, leaving the door open for a return trip.

*

"Eighty-seven Jaguar," Gantt called out to him, sticking his head inside the office door.

"Thanks, Victor," he called back, before the guy took off down the hallway.

"What'd he do, buy a new car?" Peterson asked, playing with the computer.

"It's what Wheeler drives," he answered, fumbling through his briefcase to retrieve Gantt's list of cars.

Peterson turned his attention from the computer screen to see him scanning the list. From the flat expression on his face, it was difficult to tell whether he was intrigued or annoyed with the attention Adam was giving it.

"Is it in there?" he asked, tipping his hand to his interest.

He held his reply until he completed the scanning. "Nope, I'm afraid not," Adam said, tossing his pen and pad onto the desk. "I could have sworn his car would have been among them."

"Any cabs?" Peterson asked.

"None on the northbound lane."

"Buses?"

"One, but I'm sure it wouldn't have stopped to let her off in the middle of the bridge. Besides, cabs and buses allow too much time for a potential jumper to rethink their intention."

"The quicker the better," Peterson said, pushing up from the chair to stretch his back and letting out a groan as he did. "There is another scenario, you know."

"What's that?" Adam asked.

"A man who cheats on his wife, particularly if the wife happens to be the niece of a sheriff, is likely to take precautions," Peterson said, alternately bending his torso to the side and back. "I don't need to tell you I've been involved in the investigation of many a cheating spouse. Not too surprisingly, they don't care to be seen cruising around town with the other woman perched in their front seat. So, what do they do to cut down on the odds of them being spotted, especially if they are driving an easily recognizable Jaguar? I'll tell you what they do…they cough up the cash for a rental car."

It was an obvious point that never occurred to him.

"A wasted trip is what you're saying?"

"Nope, not at all," Peterson replied, ending his calisthenics and plopping his body back down into the chair. "The process of elimination is a fundamental strategy of the trade. You've narrowed the options. Now you need to whittle them down more."

Peterson hoisted the yellow pages from the desk onto his lap and fanned through the listings. "Let's start with the big ones," he said, drawing a finger down a page with one hand while picking up the phone and punching a number with the other.

Here he goes again with the phone routine, Adam thought, curious as to his boss's intent.

"—Yes, Monte Wheeler here, could you punch up my name on your computer there for me? I rented a car from you people a while back, around May 7, I believe. I tell you I was so impressed with the car's performance I'm now thinking of purchasing one for myself. I just wanted to verify the exact make of the car—you don't have my name listed—Wheeler—Monte—right—you know, I may have dialed the wrong rental agency. Thank you for your trouble."

He immediately punched in the next number, leaning back in

his chair like he was in it for the long haul.

"—Yes—Monte Wheeler here—could you punch up my name on your computer there—"

The script and the results were the same for the next five contacts, yet the pattern failed to deter him.

"—Yes…Monte Wheeler here," he said for a sixth time, reciting the lines as if he was the immediate supervisor of the person on the other end of the end of the telephone line.

"Wheeler—yes—Monte—right—you did find the listing," he said, sitting upright in his chair. "May 6th I rented it—sounds right—'87 blue Olds Cutlass—that's it—yes—it was a dandy. I certainly appreciate your help. Have a good day."

Peterson hung up the phone and closed the phone book with a flick of the wrist. "Eighty-seven blue Cutlass, in case you didn't hear," he said with a glint in his eye to his new hire across the desk. "Rented it the day before."

Adam quickly checked his notes. An instant later he was on the phone to Gantt, arranging a hurry-up return trip to the DOT office for a second viewing.

"By the way, my wife and I would like to have you over for dinner Monday evening," Peterson said on his way out the door. "Say around six? That is if you don't have any classes to make."

"No, I'm free. But tell her not to go to any great trouble."

"Believe me, she won't. Cooking comes easy for her. How does baked chicken and rice sound?"

"Anything beats boil-in-the-bags," he called to his boss, already halfway out the door.

*

"There it is!" Gantt said from the edge of his seat, pointing to the blue Olds crawling toward the toll plaza behind a Chevy convertible.

"Can you stop it the moment it reaches the gate?" he asked.

"Okay, okay, there," Gantt said, hitting the pause button before pushing back his chair from the video stand.

For a moment they sat in silence, studying the frozen screen.

"Can you forward it a bit to show him paying the toll?" he asked.

Gantt leaned forward to punch the play button. Seconds later a man's hand reached out the car window to pass the toll to the attendant.

"Exact change," he said, as the car advanced past the booth.

"Meaning what?" Gantt asked.

"Meaning nothing," he replied.

He checked Gantt's list drawn from the day before to see how far down the Cutlass was listed.

"Let's let it run to the point where my truck shows up, so we can determine the time interval between him and me," he said.

Fifteen minutes later his pickup came into the picture.

"Okay, you can stop it."

He checked the list again.

"About sixty cars between the two of us," he said. "Now, let's put in the tape from the southbound toll plaza. I want to see how many, if any of these cars passed him on the bridge."

Gantt slipped in another tape and ran it to the time the Olds appeared at the northbound gate.

"Okay, let it roll," he said.

He followed the string of cars, patiently checking from his list the number that passed the Olds from one gate to the other.

"Twenty vehicles beat him across the bridge," he eventually announced to Gantt. "It means he slowed considerably, or more likely came to a momentary stop."

"It also means he was only forty or so cars ahead of you when he took off again," Gantt said.

"Maybe what, five or ten minutes to the time I came upon her?"

"Somewhere in there."

It was a much shorter interval than he expected, but plenty of time for Charlene to have exited the car in one manner or the other and then walk to the bridge railing.

"Do you suppose the cops went through this exercise?" Gantt asked, removing the tape from the machine.

"I doubt it. They had little motivation to do so. For one thing, there were no family members around to pressure them into a full-blown investigation. Secondly, it was deemed a suicide, which meant the media was not going to be pushing them."

"What's pushing you, Adam?" the insurance man asked in turn.

He shrugged. He already had asked himself the same question and discovered he had no good answer.

CHAPTER FIVE

Jill Peterson, a petite woman of intelligent look and modest beauty, cast a comfortable presence about her, much like her husband. The combination made for a relaxed dinner atmosphere, as did their home, a sizable cream-colored villa with a burnt-orange tile roof arching over an interior replete with reupholstered furniture, glass-topped tables, and Indian rugs scattered across laminate wooden floors.

"Are you sure you don't care for an after-dinner drink?" Jill asked from a love seat she shared with her husband.

"No thank you; the dinner wine was plenty enough for me," Adam responded, slumped in a cushy armchair.

"Pete tells me you're interested in pursuing a career as a PI," she said, adjusting a comb, binding the knob of light brown hair she had drawn tight from her slender face.

"I've been considering it," he said.

"He's considering getting in, while we're considering getting out," her husband chimed in, releasing his arm from around his wife's shoulders to place his drink on an end table.

"We're thinking of retiring and opening up a scrimshaw shop down in the Keys," she said in explanation.

"Yeah, you'd never guess, would you?" her husband asked, circling his eyes around the room.

Arranged on tables large and small throughout the home were pieces of the craft as well as framed paintings of it on the living room walls.

He picked up one of the pieces from an end table, a whale's tooth, and scanned its fanciful design.

"Pete became interested in it years ago after purchasing a piece from an underwater treasure hunter in the Caribbean. We've been collecting ever since."

"It looks as though you already have enough stock to open up a shop," he observed.

"Oh, this isn't all of it," his boss quickly said. "We've got closets full in the back."

"Must be a valuable collection," he said, wondering if the comment was appropriate. It was the reason he tried to avoid social gatherings whenever possible. He was no good at small talk.

"Your neighbor downtown, Victor Gantt, gave us a nice deal on the insurance, so we can breathe a little easier in that regard," she said.

"Not that anyone would break into this place," her husband cracked with a wink.

"I'm also trying to talk Pete into taking up boating, since we'll be surrounded by water down there," she said.

"I've lived in Florida my entire life and been out on a boat once and once was enough," her husband responded.

"Bad experience?" Adam asked.

"A strange one," Jill said, turning to her husband in expectation of an explanation.

"A couple we know invited us out for a little fishing trip on their boat," he said. "Well, we're sitting out there in the hot sun for God knows how long and not getting a bite when this stingray suddenly comes shooting straight out of the water and into the boat, landing on my lap. Scared the crap out of me. Here I'm one of those guys who shuffles his feet along the beach to make sure he doesn't get stung and look what happens—one lands in my lap."

"Excuse me," Adam said, puzzled by the account. "But I wasn't aware stingrays could fly."

"Same thing I said to our fishing partners," Peterson said. "They blamed it on *Flipper*. Said porpoises are known to play with stingrays—flip them into the air for fun. Can you believe it? The only time I'm out on a boat and I'm hit by a flying fish."

"What happened to the stingray?" Adam asked.

"After I jumped about ten feet, he landed on the deck. We wrapped him in a towel and heaved him back in. We then sat for ten minutes staring at the still water, expecting *Flipper* to flip him back to us, but I guess he got tired of the game."

"He won't even go on a cruise with me," his wife said.

"Yeah, getting away from it all and every fifteen minutes some guy's knocking on your door announcing it's time for bingo."

"That's not true," his wife said in mock displeasure, nearly spilling her wine.

Pete turned to Adam. "Let's go on a three-week one, she says. Sure, first day out I decide I don't like it, I figure they're not about to turn around and bring me back."

"Well then, as a test run, let's try one of those single-day cruises out of the Port of Tampa I've been telling you about," she said. "I hear the passage under the Sunshine Skyway at night on the return trip is spectacular, a perfect time for trying out my new camera."

"No thanks. I'd rather take my chances on dry land chasing down bad guys than getting spooked by sea creatures."

"You never had a desire to go into law enforcement, Adam?" his wife asked, giving her husband a breather.

"I've considered it but I've had enough experience with the enforcement end of it in the Air Force to learn I'd prefer the gumshoe aspect of it."

Pete turned to his wife. "Right now he's wearing a pair of shoes out, tracking the suicide case I was telling you about."

"Such a sad situation," she said, shaking her head. "What more can you do, Adam?"

He glanced at his boss. "For one thing, I've been thinking about giving Monte Wheeler a visit."

Peterson stalled his drink at his lips. "Oh, yeah?"

"Yes. I'll tell him I'm taking a journalism class and as part of the course would like to interview an executive editor."

"What would you discuss with him?" Jill asked, folding her legs underneath her pleated lavender skirt.

"The principals and principles of a story," he said, having given it some thought.

"The principals and principles of a story," she repeated. "Hmm…interesting. You're relating this to the Charlene Gibbs story, I presume?"

"I would hope so," her husband interjected. "He's at a stage where the pot needs to be stirred. Besides, the press doesn't like to be pressed. They're similar to the basketball team that likes to full-court press but when faced with a press, falls apart. Unless, of course, they have a Hook-n Ladder Hooper on their team to break it," he said, reaching out and tapping his wife on the knee.

She pressed her forehead with the palm of her hand. "Oh no, here we go again."

"Who's Hook-n Ladder Hooper?" Adam could not resist asking.

"You shouldn't have asked," Jill said.

Her husband jumped to his feet, as if given the go-ahead, and stood in the middle of the living room, loosening his long-sleeved shirt and tie.

"I'll tell you who he was, Adam. He was this kid who played center on our high school basketball squad. The guy was seven-feet tall and whenever an opposing team would press us, our coach would position Hooper near the in-bounds line and have the guy passing the ball in toss it high to him. He then would turn and pass it down court to a teammate for a breakaway lay-up. His other job was to roam under the basket on offense where we would feed him the ball for little hook shots. I tell you the guy hardly ever took a dribble during an entire game, just loped up and down the court with his gangling arms raised high."

Peterson was taking giant steps up and down the living room floor, mimicking his former teammate. He looked like Groucho Marx striding back and forth without the cigar.

"That's enough!" his wife exclaimed, her hand covering her mouth to stifle the giggles. "You're going to knock over something if you aren't careful."

Peterson ended his act, rejoining his wife on the loveseat. "No, I guarantee you the *Beacon* has no Hook-n Ladder Hooper to beat the press," he said, taking a sip of wine.

"I think this is going to be more of a probe than a press, Pete," Adam said, lowering the levity in the room.

"Honey, do you think Adam has the experience to be taking on such a weighty matter?" Mrs. Peterson bluntly asked. "It's not the kind of case I would expect a new hire to be handed."

"Hey, I didn't assign him the case. In fact, it's not even on the company agenda. It's strictly volunteer stuff," he said. "Not that I object, since it is damn good experience for him. There's something to be said for throwing a kid in the pool to get him to swim."

Jill Peterson cast a dumbfounded look at her husband and then at him. "When do you ever find time for a social life?"

"Oh, there you go. I knew she would slip that one in," her husband said. "What she really wants to know is if you have a girlfriend."

"Pete, I meant no such thing," she replied, smiling through her sea-green eyes.

"You're right, Mrs. Peterson. I haven't had much time for a social life, since getting out of the service," he said, hoping to deflect the discussion.

"He tells me about all these young coeds at school and how he feels like an old Methuselah among them," Pete continued to his chagrin. "What's the name of the honey who sits next to you in your journalism class; the one who seems to have taken interest in you?"

"Eva," he murmured.

"Yeah, Eva. Adam and Eva—I like it," Peterson went on, directing his words to his wife who appeared bemused by her husband's interest in his employee's private life.

"Every five minutes the gal leans over and grabs his—what is it she grabs?" he asked, turning from his wife to him.

"Touches my forearm," he said, unable to hold back a chuckle.

"Yeah, grabs a forearm to ask him what page of the text they are on. Every five minutes she does it. What does that tell you?"

"What page we are on," he deadpanned.

"For crying out loud, you're hopeless, Adam," he said, waving his hand in a dismissive manner. "Believe me, someday you'll regret passing Eva up."

"You make it sound like it's a sure thing," he said.

"Hey, if it's rejection you're worried about, don't be. It's part of life whether you're selling cars or yourself," Pete said. "Back in my younger days, I had a buddy who wasn't exactly what you would call a ladies man, but he didn't let it stop him from playing the game. His theory was if the first twenty women turned him down for a dance or a date, the twenty-first would say yes."

"I'm not so sure I could handle rejection as well as he did," Adam said.

"Maybe Adam doesn't care to be distracted in class," his wife said, coming to his defense. "Maybe he's there to learn."

"Sure, speaking of class, don't forget I signed you up for the Ronnie Weeks surveillance training seminar this Friday over at the Bay Tower Inn," he said, finally changing the subject. "He may be a competitor of mine but the guy's damn good—knows all the ins and outs of the legal hurdles, which is must-have learning in our business. It's almost gotten to the point nowadays where you have to have a licensed lawyer tailing you around while you're on the tail of someone else."

"It's not only in the private eye business but the scrimshaw trade as well," his wife added.

"Lots of legal restrictions awaiting you there, too?" Adam asked, making conversation.

"For sure," she said. "In some cases selling whale bone and teeth can land you in trouble with the law quicker than selling illegal drugs. The Endangered Species Act changed everything. Now the scrimshaw practitioners have to rely on materials coming from extinct animals, or materials shed naturally from animals like moose antlers, or materials derived from animals of old, like billiard balls…"

And so it went the remainder of the evening, with talk of walrus tusks, elephant ivory, whale teeth, deer antlers, cattle horns, and the historical handcraft practiced on them. Yet, amid all the discussion of ancient mariners and Yankee sailors, Adam came away from the evening with one overriding impression: the anchor in Pete Peterson's life was not his current profession or profession-to-be, but his wife. For sure, his boss had chosen wisely and for that he should be thankful. He left, hoping the fates would be as kind to him.

*

"Oh, to be a fly on that wall," Peterson cracked over the phone when Adam informed him he was headed for the *Beacon* Building to see if he could arrange a spur-of-the-moment meeting with Wheeler. "Be sure and let me know how it goes down."

*

The Beacon Building rose from the center of the downtown district like a monolith, a three-story structure spanning an entire block. A dull peach in color, its art deco exterior was dominated by giant panes of transparent tinted glass, giving it an open-air appearance designed to project an open-access image to the community.

Immediately upon entering the building, he walked to a reception counter adjoining the lobby where a wafer-thin, curly-haired brunette in a green polka dot dress was shuffling papers from one wire basket to the other while keeping an eye out for arriving guests.

"May I help you?" she asked, brushing aside a stray curl from her forehead.

"Yes, I would like to see Monte Wheeler, if I may."

She turned and looked past clusters of computer-topped desks, some occupied, some not, to a glass-enclosed office planted in the center of the room. Inside it, a lone figure appeared to be at work at his desk.

"Did you have an appointment?" she asked.

"No, but since I was downtown anyway, I thought I'd try my luck and catch him while he's not busy," Adam said, gesturing towards the editor's office.

"May I tell him what this is about?" she asked, resting a hand on a counter phone.

"Yes. I am a journalism student at Live Oak Community College. As part of my class preparation, I would like to ask him a few questions regarding the profession."

She picked up the receiver and punched a number. Instantly, the figure in the glass-enclosed office reached for the phone.

"Mr. Wheeler, this is Shari at the front desk. There is a man here who is a student at Live Oak Community College. He would like to speak with you. It's regarding the journalism profession—no, I don't think he's looking for a job."

She glanced at Adam for verification and he shook his head no.

"…right…okay," she said, replacing the receiver. "Mr. Wheeler has some business to tend to. He may or may not be able to get to you," she said somewhat apologetically. "You're welcome to have a seat," she added as a courtesy, while motioning to an elongated red leather bench braced against a wall.

There he waited, eating up minutes like he ate up lima beans, slowly and determinedly. Fifteen minutes passed, then thirty. Meanwhile, people scurried in and out of the building and in and out of Wheeler's office. At times, the receptionist would glance at him sitting patiently on the bench, angle her head to take another look at the glass cage, see her boss prowling it with phone in hand, and then turn back to him with a wan smile and shrug. In response, he took out some notes from his journalism class to review. Another half hour passed with still no summons from the receptionist. By now her impatience, whether directed at him or her boss, was showing. She again turned to face the glass cage, saw Wheeler back at his desk, picked up the phone, punched a number, whispered a message, and nodded her head a few times, before wheeling back around and hanging up the receiver.

"Mr. Wheeler will see you now," she said with a measure of relief.

She swung open a counter door, allowing him passage into the newsroom. Time would tell if the wait was worth it, he told himself, as he brushed between rows of cluttered desks to the see-through office.

"Hey, you must be the journalism guy," Wheeler said as way of introduction. "Have a chair."

He took one directly across from the editor, fumbling for a scratch pad from his briefcase as he did.

"I'll be with you in a moment," Wheeler said, clicking his computer mouse a few final times, before swinging his black leather executive chair around to face him directly for the first time. "Now what is it I can do for you?" he asked in a voice as detached as his demeanor, not bothering to ask his visitor for a name.

He displayed the classic square face of anyone called Rock, a granite shape from jaw to forehead with strong eyebrows arching over steady brown eyes. Even his close-clipped rusty hair had a chiseled look to it.

"Thank you for taking the time out from your schedule to see me. As part of my class preparation, I thought it would be beneficial to get an editor's perspective on the state of the profession today," he said, narrowing down what he told the receptionist. "So, I drew up a few questions I would like to ask you, if you don't mind."

Wheeler gave him a listless shrug of the shoulders, as if he did.

He glanced at the scratch pad on his lap. "Okay, as an executive editor, what do you consider the profession's primary responsibility?"

Wheeler again shrugged. "As a practical matter, it's very simple. It's to assemble and verify facts," he said in rote fashion

"And in your position as executive editor, what do you see as your primary responsibility?"

He wrinkled his brow. "I have a number of responsibilities," he replied, but if I had to narrow them down to one, I would say it was to first identify the informational needs of the community we serve and to see to it they are addressed in a timely manner."

Wheeler casually picked up a handwritten note from his desk, glanced at it, and set it aside next to a framed color photograph of a fresh-faced young woman with thick auburn hair streaming down across her shoulders. The sheriff's niece, Adam presumed.

"By community, you mean all segments of it?" he asked as a follow-up.

"Yes, of course," he said, making a show of checking his watch. "We don't want any segment of our readership to feel disenfranchised."

He drew his finger down his pad to the next question. "Who then is the editor's primary allegiance to—the company, the advertisers, or the public?"

"No question, to the citizens. Once you earn their trust and loyalty, the economic benefits fall in line."

The desk phone buzzed and Wheeler quickly snatched it. "Yes, Shari...right...right...I know. I'll be finished in a couple of minutes," he said, wedging the receiver between his shoulder and ear to brush some lint from the front of his starched blue dress shirt and bold red tie.

He hung up the phone and again glanced at his watch. "Can we hurry this along? The governor is in town and I'm scheduled to appear at a public forum with him in an hour."

"Sure. I'm down to my final question, anyway," he said, flipping a page of the notebook he was reading from. "Okay, what would you say makes for a good journalist?"

"A good nose for a story," he pointedly said. "Other than that, I'd say a mind for accuracy and seeing to it that all leads are followed through on. And, oh yes, a willingness to maintain a sense of proportion by not leaving important elements out of a story."

Adam nodded his head. "We're often reminded in class of the old admonition not to become part of the story," he said on finding his opening. "How does a journalist avoid doing so?"

"By keeping an independent state of mind," Wheeler said. "I have often stated we are like appointed judges in this regard. In fact, I would have no objection if a reporter asked to be withdrawn from a story, if he or she felt they could not maintain an objective distance from it, okay?" The "okay" meant Wheeler was running out of patience with Adam.

He checked off his last question and leaned back in his chair. "If I may, one follow-up relating to what you said about leaving items out of a story," he said, reaching into his briefcase to pull out a newspaper clipping. "It has to do with this story you ran a while back on a young woman who jumped to her death from the Sunshine Skyway Bridge."

Wheeler's restless eyes suddenly locked on him like radar on an approaching missile, as if sensing one was about to strike him square between the pupils.

"From what I understand, she had a sister who was killed in the collapse of the old Sunshine Skyway Bridge seven years ago.

There was no mention of this in the *Beacon* story," he said, holding the article aloft, while attempting to keep a steady hand.

The editor's eyes narrowed, burrowing into his with an intensity words apparently could not convey, even in the vocabulary of a seasoned journalist. Undoubtedly, he realized his guest inquisitor knew there was more to the story than what appeared in the paper, so why let him continue?

"Are you one of those professional students, the guys who hang around the lounges solving the world's problems without getting their hands dirty?" Wheeler asked, holding in his ire. "You do look a little old for college life."

And here Adam thought his four years in the service allowed him time to mature a little, given him some legs to stand on, provided a perspective on life he otherwise would have lacked if had gone straight from high school to college.

"I got a late start."

"What did you say your name was?"

"I didn't."

"Well, Mr. Whatever-Your-Name is, I think it is time for you to leave," he said, a sardonic smile forming at the corners of his mouth. "I suggest you go back to your class or student lounge and learn a little more about matters of personal privacy, before you come waltzing in here again."

Adam offered no comeback, no witty rejoinder. Instead, he casually placed his notepad back into his briefcase and left the editor's office with nary a parting word. He continued to feel the editor's eyes burning into his back as he crossed through the newsroom, past a smiling, unaware Shari, and out the front door, all the while pondering whether he had just become part of the story.

*

"I can picture it now," Peterson said, framing his hands in the air. "Wheeler at his glass wall, frantically attempting to form a peephole by wiping away the steam you and he created and then staring daggers at your back, as you calmly stroll out the door."

"It wasn't quite that dramatic, Pete. In fact, I'm not sure the whole thing amounted to much, other than to tick him off."

"You stirred the pot," Peterson said. "What else could you do? Wait around for a public confession on his part?"

"I'm convinced he drove her to the bridge," Adam said.

"Oh, so you're going to try and get the cops to nail him on some kind of assisted suicide charge? Maybe charge him for leaving the scene of one, if there is such a thing?"

"Did you know that in Elizabethan times a widow or widower marrying their brother-in-law or sister-in-law was considered incest?"

His boss eyed him from over his water bottle, as he finished gulping down a mouthful. "First of all, he didn't marry her. Secondly, if you think he's ripe for a charge of incest, think again."

"It's not a crime I'm chasing, it's a story," he said. "There's one to be told."

"Great. The fledgling private investigator is turning journalist on me," Peterson snapped. "You're becoming more the college freshman every passing day, the one who can't make up his mind what career path he wants to follow, so he winds up going every which way until he ends up lost."

"When you come right down to it, aren't both professions in the snooping business?"

"Yes, but remember, when two snoops start butting heads, it's the one with the most weight behind him who ends up on his feet."

"Meaning?"

"Meaning one guy has an institution, a pillar of the community behind him. The other has a cubby hole of an office with bad air conditioning."

He let out a breath in reaction to the comparison. "If I recall right, it was you who was all in favor of stirring the pot."

"Okay, you've stirred it. Time to probe in a different direction. If you think somebody did somebody wrong, you first need to establish what the harm was and go from there," Peterson said. "It seems to me, Adam, you're dealing more in newspaper ethics or moral issues than potential criminal activity at this point."

"And if there is no criminal activity?" he asked his boss.

"Then the story ends here."

CHAPTER SIX

In the PI business there are times when it is better to be heard than seen, Adam's boss would say, better to sidle along in the shadows than strut in the sun, better to work the phones than fly the firm's flag in person, which was why Adam was on the line to the sheriff's office trying to track down someone in the know regarding events of seven years past.

"What exactly is it you're after?" the robotic voice on the other end asked.

"I'd like to speak to someone who might have knowledge of the events surrounding the collapse of the old Skyway Bridge, specifically the procedures followed in notifying the families of those killed in the incident."

"Hang on."

Adam propped his feet up on a kitchen chair across from where he was sitting and took another bite out of a cold meat loaf sandwich he was having for lunch. As he waited, he listened to the soft beat of reggae music wafting up and in from a neighbor's patio below.

"Did you try the morgue or medical examiner's office?" the voice asked, coming back on the line.

"Both of them with no luck. They referred me to you."

"Just a moment," he said, his testiness level rising.

Two more bites out of his sandwich and the sheriff's guy was back on the phone again. "What's this for?"

"I'm a student doing a class research paper on government emergency procedures and I chose the Skyway Bridge collapse as my topic."

"Well, we talked it over here and think your best bet is to talk to a gal by the name of Martha Winstead. She was coordinating many of the post-accident activities. Trouble is, she retired a couple of years ago."

"Do you have any idea how I could get in touch with her?"

"Hey Judy! Do you know where this fellow could get in touch with Martha?" he barked.

Adam finished his sandwich listening to the guy chatter with his colleague in the background.

"We can't give you her home phone or address. However, I'm told she does volunteer work for the Greater Cause Thrift Shop over on Stratford Square. You might catch her there," he eventually growled over the line. As soon as Adam got off the phone, he checked the directory for the thrift shop's number and dialed it. A recorded message came on announcing the staff was out to lunch and would be back on duty at one o'clock. Rather than wait around to dial again, he decided to make a visit to the store, feeling she might be reluctant to speak to him at any length over the phone for fear of tying up the line.

Minutes later he was steering his truck through one of Tampa's oldest neighborhoods, a section of town yet to be impacted by the gentrification movement triggered by the recent influx of young professionals to the central city. In time the area would be targeted, but for now he was traveling a well-worn path, down scarred streets lined with concrete-block houses and weathered clapboard duplexes. Ultimately the path led him to a pockmarked parking lot, connecting sidewalk, and an unattached sandstone building the size of a bowling alley.

A cardboard open-for-business sign hung crooked in the door window, signaling lunch was over. Upon entering, he was greeted by the jingle of a bell dangling by a ribbon from the inside doorknob. Immediately, an elderly woman stuck her head out from between two racks of women's dresses. She dispensed with welcoming words, giving him first say.

He carefully closed the door behind him, so not to disturb the bell. "Are you Martha Winstead?"

"Yes?"

She carried the features of a frontier woman, lean and leathered face with clear blue eyes and gray hair rolled up tight in a bun. Somewhat surprising for a woman cooped up in government offices for all these years, he thought.

He introduced himself, explaining in general terms the purpose of his visit. It was enough to coax her into agreeing to talk; something she seemed predisposed to do. Like every veteran he had ever known, military or otherwise, she had war stories she was anxious to tell. The store was nearly empty of customers as it was, plus she had an assistant to boot, a rawboned woman with curly dark brown hair and pasty complexion to help monitor the floor in case business picked up.

He trailed her down a narrow aisle, dodging domestic odds and ends crowded onto tables. The store almost could be divided by scent, he mused—the mothball fragrance indicating the clothing aisle—the musty odor signaling the old books section, and so on. Altogether, it coalesced into the familiar thrift-store smell, bringing back memories of his forays into the attic of his boyhood home to dig out family relics.

"This is a good place to sit," she said, gesturing to a hand-me-down table and two chairs nestled in a back corner of the room.

She settled in across from him. "Now, where would you like for me to start? From the first Mayday?"

"Yes, from the first Mayday, if you could," he said, readily agreeing to her timetable.

She wiped her hands across a pale blue apron covering her dark denim blouse and skirt and rested them together on the table. "It was the start of a hectic day, believe me," she said in a strong voice. "The ship's harbor pilot was radioing in the Mayday as soon as he realized what had happened. He made clear right off there were multiple bodies in the water. Still, we had no idea of the scope of the disaster until the first emergency crews arrived on the scene. Only then did the magnitude of it hit us. We realized we were faced with a major tragedy, not the one-or-two fatality case we were accustomed to. A number of vehicles were reported in the water and tangled up in the wreckage of the bridge, including a bus, which was turned upside down on the surface and split wide open."

She paused a moment to shake her head. "One of our men brought back some early photos of the scene. It looked like a graveyard had been flushed to the surface with all of the bodies and debris floating around," she said. "I was told a gray mist was hanging low over the bay, to make it appear even more eerie. In addition, part of the Skyway's roadway ended up on the bow of the freighter, which must have spooked the ship's crew to no end. The man who took the photos said you could hear the twisted steel wreckage creaking and groaning in the aftermath."

"Can't imagine how the pilot must have felt," he said.

Her eyes widened. "How would you feel standing at the helm of an out-of-control freighter six-hundred feet long and eighty feet wide in a channel four-hundred feet wide and be faced with navigating the underside of the Skyway in that kind of storm? Talk about trying to thread a needle. From what I heard, the ship was bobbing like a cork in the water."

"Don't they build those bridges with any kind of protection?" Adam asked, trying to recall if he ever noticed anything of the kind in his travels over it.

"They had wooden barriers on the old bridge, which were

designed to protect it against a collision, but the salt water ate most of them away over time. The new bridge has massive protection, as you might expect following the earlier fiasco."

"Barriers?"

"Large, circular, concrete ones," she said, motioning wide with her hands.

"Must have been a monumental public relations headache for you following the collision," he said.

"For me and everyone else directly involved," she said. "We knew from past experience and planning how important it was to have accurate identification from the medical examiner's office before we started notifying families. Passing out inaccurate information is worse than providing no information at all. As you can imagine, the moment the news crews came on the scene and began broadcasting from the site, all hell broke loose in our office. The phone lines became jammed with callers wanting to know if one of their loved ones was among the victims."

"How soon were you able to start the identification process?" he asked.

"Right away in some cases. In others it took longer. Sadly, it required days to locate some victims. The rescue crews were facing all sorts of difficulties, including the presence of sharks in the area, which prevented the divers from immediately entering the waters. By the time the rescue operation was finally completed, we ended up contacting relatives from as far away as Canada."

"What is involved in the identification process?"

"Depending on the circumstances, there are a number of factors to consider," she said, as if preparing to recite from a government procedural manual she had referred to countless times on the job. "For one thing, we rely to a great extent on people calling to let us know who is missing. If we are fortunate, we obtain a piece of identification off of the victim…a driver's license, social security number, something along those lines. We also check dental records, fingerprints, dimple charts, and photos of bodies. If none of these procedures work, we end up checking for rings, necklaces, tattoos—anything on the body that will provide us a positive identification. By the way, the recovery of personal belongings is very important to the families, even if it is only a single item. They often view it as their last tie to the victim."

As she spoke a shaft of sunlight broke through an opening in the partially closed blinds of a nearby window, illuminating her weathered face, deeply lined by years of experience and responsibility.

"I imagine the notification process took considerable time," he said.

"You bet it did. But like I said, our first task was to make sure the information we gathered was correct. Unfortunately, in major disasters like this, some families receive their information through the media and what they get is not always current or correct. Then you have the lawyers entering the picture, which raises a whole other set of problems."

"Entering when and where?"

She cleared her throat softly. "Well, often the initial reaction of family members to hearing the death of a loved one is to immediately head for the scene of an accident. They almost feel compelled to do so, feeling it is a way of honoring and saying goodbye to the victims. For them it represents the beginning of the healing process. Regrettably, there often are a few overzealous attorneys on the scene who don't mind approaching them with business cards in hand. The arrival of relatives also presents problems for the law enforcement officers at the site. They have to make sure visiting families are not given access to bodies or personal belongings before they are checked by medical examiners. The other thing we have to watch out for is the language we use in addressing the families. No mention is to be made of body parts, body pieces, body fragments, or dismembered bodies. Instead, we are to refer to the severe condition of the body or the trauma to the body."

"Considering the shock they were in following the Skyway incident, I would think they would not recall much at all of what was said to them."

"True, and as often is the case, they misunderstand what they are hearing, which can lead to difficulties later on."

"I know of a young woman who went down with the bus," he said, abruptly slipping in an item he did not mention in his introduction.

"Do you now," she said, tweaked by his revelation. "What was her name?"

"Carlene Wheeler," he said. "Do you recall her?"

"Excuse me Martha, a customer wants to know if he can have this toaster for five dollars," her assistant called from across the way, holding up the item. "It's listed for seven but five is all he has on him."

"That's fine Mildred. Let him have it," she said, looking over her shoulder.

"Sorry," she said, returning her attention to him. "What was the name again you were asking about?"

"Carlene Wheeler."

"Carlene Wheeler...oh yes, I recall her name. She was one of the first victims to be recovered and identified."

"About what time was that?" he asked, sounding like a courtroom lawyer.

"Later in the day...evening sometime. She was found with her handbag twisted around her body as I recall, so we were able to retrieve several pieces of identification off her."

"You had the job of contacting her husband?"

"Yes, but as I remember we did run into a hitch in her case. Normally, we try to send out uniformed officers to notify victims' families, which is what we did in her situation. However, no one was at home, so we resorted to the phone. Fortunately, she had an emergency call list on her with listings for her husband and sister. I called his home first but there was no answer, only a request on his answering machine to leave a message. Well, that is something we prefer not to do. There are horror stories aplenty of victims' families being left with impersonal messages on their answering machines, notifying them of a loved one's death. Believe me, you don't want to be leaving a message saying 'your wife is on ice at the morgue.' Know what I mean?"

"Yes," Adam said , suppressing a smile. "So what did you do?"

"I then called his work number. I recall this well because it turned out he was a big shot at the *Beacon*, as you might know. As a result, I fully expected him to be aware of the disaster, if not his wife's death. However, I was told he was not at work. He had taken the day off and, no, they didn't know where he was."

"Did you tell them what it was you were calling about?"

"No. I didn't want him to receive the information second hand, so I went to the next name on her emergency list…her sister. I believe her name was Dobbs or Hobbs or something similar."

"Gibbs—Charlene Gibbs."

"Yes…Gibbs, that's it. Anyway, I called and she answered immediately. I asked if she knew where I might get in touch with her brother-in-law, thinking at the time there was little chance of her knowing. Well, after hesitating a bit, she surprised me by saying he's right here and handing the phone over to him. I then knew there was no other option but to tell him of the tragedy, since it was senseless to try and arrange a personal visit at that stage of the process."

"What was his reaction?"

"Shock, of course. 'Carlene killed!' he said. As soon as he did, I heard the sister gasp 'What?' in the background. After giving them a moment to settle down, I gave him some of the details and informed him of where he could locate her body and personal belongings."

"Like you indicated, it is interesting he was in the news business and yet was not aware of the tragedy," he said.

"Yes, and it was all over the radio and television," she said.

"I guess they didn't have either on," he said.

"No, they sure didn't, though I did hear music going in the background," she said almost as an afterthought. "In fact, when she first came on the line, she asked him to turn it down, so she could hear me."

"Interesting," Adam said.

"Yes, and I remember exactly what was playing, one of my all-time favorites, Frank Sinatra's *The Summer Wind*. Strange, isn't it?"

"Yeah…strange," he said, believing otherwise.

*

Adam went for a drive. He took his textbooks and set out for Ballast Point Park to while away the remainder of the day under a shade tree, reading and taking in a Florida sunset. Instead of sticking his head in the textbooks, however, he stuck it in the clouds, letting it float wherever his whims might take it. Invariably, it was back to the woman who launched him on his present journey. So she may have been involved in a tawdry relationship with her brother-in-law. What business was it of his? They were consenting adults, after all. Were they not?

He watched the fishermen lined up along the railings of the pier cast their lines into the bay below where the salt waters of the sea mingled freely with the fresh waters of the rivers. It is here they produce a wonder of their own, an underwater world filled with strange and familiar creatures living side by side in a fragile harmony. As a child Adam's father made it a weekend ritual to take him to the coast for some pier fishing. It marked his first exposure to the sea, a baby step into a world too giant for his Lilliputian mind to fully fathom. He recalled the stops at the bait shop at the foot of the pier where he would hang his chin over the edges of the metal tanks to watch the darting minnows and sardines move in graceful unison. On the walls of the bait shop were mounted large black and white photos of people of all ages, shapes, and sizes hoisting their catches high for the eye of the camera. In his mind's eye he dreamed of the day his photograph would hang among them. The best he could do was a five-pound sea bass, which his father to his glee asked him to hold aloft for a photo. It later made it onto the wall of the family den next to a framed photo of his father's high school football jersey and his mother's ballet shoes.

By and by, a shorebird cackled above wresting him back to the present. Far in the distance a cruise ship, silhouetted by the setting sun, inched its way toward the horizon. He followed its image, a living seascape eventually lulling him into a sleep, away from the hard reality of the day and of the morrows.

CHAPTER SEVEN

If the small sampling of attendees he met at the surveillance seminar was any indication, then Pete Peterson, a private investigator for nearly his entire professional life, was one of a kind. For the most part, they were former cops, military vets, or industrial security personnel. Ronnie Weeks was no exception. An ex-special operations officer with the Army, he presented an imposing figure at the podium. Tall and lean, with a ruddy face and a generous helping of white hair, he spoke in a throaty voice requiring minimal acoustical assistance.

His very presence stood at odds with his primary admonition of not calling attention to one's self. "It may seem like the computer has done you a favor by switching your workplace from the seat of your automobile to the seat of your office, but don't be fooled," he said. "Yes, it's true you no longer have to live in your car and worry about running the air conditioner hours on end. I'm sure you're all familiar with that scene—fighting to stay awake—the soft drink cans and paper cups scattered on the floorboard—the empty packs of cigarettes. However, the big payoffs still come from the legwork, the documentation of real-time human behavior in support of your client." He then proceeded to tackle the ticklish issue of the right to privacy as it applied to surveillance techniques. "If nothing else, you must recognize the difference between peeking through hedges into a private home and lawful listening and observation. Yes, the public has a right to privacy and we have a right to investigate, as long as we abide by the rules. Just be careful with exercising rights. Remember, you also have a right to walk through Harlem in the middle of the night waving the Confederate flag, but I wouldn't recommend it."

Despite the daylong concentration on legal and liability issues, it was a segment called "Situational Assessment" that captured Adam's interest, for it was Weeks speaking from years of personal experience. Often, he would depart from his prepared text, step to the side of the podium, prop an elbow on its side, hook a thumb under his belt, and offer anecdotes illustrating "mistakes I made you don't want to make." His biggest? They all fell under the category of leaving no stone unturned. "Far too often we are reluctant to lift the rock for fear of what we might find or who we might offend. In no way should you walk away from a situation without exploring it to its fullest. Otherwise, you may end up shortchanging your own case. Professional writers like to say writing is re-writing. Well, I'm here to tell you tailing is re-tailing, and by that I don't mean the selling of goods and services."

It was enough reason for Adam to be back on the road Saturday morning, headed north to Hidden Valley to check on a stone. A headstone. One not yet carved.

*

"It's open—come on in," the familiar voice called out from behind the door.

Pastor Conroy appeared as Adam had left him, with hands casually clasped across his lap and eyes fixed on the doorway, as though he expected his return.

"I appreciate your seeing me on such short notice," Adam said, dragging up a chair opposite the pastor.

"I thought you would have returned to Florida by now, or is this a second trip?"

"A follow-up," he said, settling into his seat.

The pastor unclasped his hands to push himself higher in the chair. "And what brings you back?"

"I'll be frank with you, Pastor Conroy. I said in our last meeting I was a friend of Charlene Gibbs. This is not exactly true, though I suppose I could be called a friend by proxy status. The truth is I only spoke to her on one occasion and it was on the bridge the evening she jumped from it. I was the sole witness to the incident."

He paused to observe a reaction, but the pastor's perplexed gaze indicated that he was awaiting further explanation.

"I work for a private investigator. I happened to be driving across the bridge at the time of the incident and attempted to intervene but with no success."

"So now you are investigating it?"

"Yes, for what reason or reasons I'm not entirely sure."

The pastor tilted his head in curiosity.

"Charlene made two comments to me before she took her life. One was 'It's where I belong.' The other was 'I hope she understands.' The first is understandable, given what we already know…"

"Her sister having been killed in the same location, you mean."

"…Yes, that's part of it but hardly the sole motivation for her. The key is in the second comment 'I hope she understands.' The question naturally arises about who is the 'she' she was referring to?"

The pastor sat in silence, but not for lack of an answer, Adam guessed.

"On my previous visit I noticed in your ledger the recording of Charlene's purchase of an additional cemetery plot. This came after her sister's death. You had mentioned the family had no intention of transferring her sister's remains to Hidden Valley, which I can understand. However, I can't help but think the plot she purchased is somehow linked to the 'she' in her final words on the bridge. Whatever else, I am convinced she uttered them as if the person was still alive."

The pastor maintained his silence, offering neither support nor objection to his conjecture, so he soldiered on.

"My boss is a very savvy individual, Pastor Conroy. He has street smarts coming out of his ears. He legitimately could preface nearly every sentence he speaks with the words 'It's been my experience.' Anyway, his explanation for Charlene's comment is a simple one, and one I second."

"And what is the explanation?" the pastor asked.

"There is a love child involved."

The old man's shoulders noticeably sagged, as if the accumulation of a career's worth of personal grievance weighing on them had finally taken its toll.

"Yes, you do have a savvy boss, Mr. Fraley," he said, after a long pause.

"Maybe not as savvy as yours," Adam responded.

The pastor momentarily raised his eyes to the ceiling, at the same time managing a wan smile.

"When Charlene returned from Tampa sometime after her sister's death, she confided in me and her parents she was pregnant. Needless to say, everyone was taken aback. She refused to say who the father was and to this day I have no idea who it may be. All I know is he's from your area. Her pregnancy was the reason for her coming home, though I understand from talking to her parents, she struggled with the decision."

"To return here?"

"Yes…out of embarrassment. After a lot of discussion and consultation, she decided to give her baby, a daughter, up for adoption."

"When was her baby born?" he asked.

"Oh…let's see…it would have been sometime in February, 1981, I believe."

"Nine months or so after her sister's death," Adam said, doing the math. "She wanted to keep her?"

"Very much. However, there were other circumstances at play which influenced her decision."

"What were those?"

The pastor reached out an unsteady hand and absentmindedly gathered scattered notes on his desk, dropping them into a trashcan.

"Not long after she returned, Charlene began to exhibit episodes of bizarre behavior, creating a lot of consternation in her parents. Eventually, she was diagnosed as bipolar.

It was hereditary, the doctor said. According to him, she probably carried the condition for years without knowing it. Usually, something traumatic triggers the affliction and in her case it was likely her sister's sudden death. It is a very debilitating disease and, sadly, resulted in her no longer being able to handle life's decisions."

"After giving up her baby, she did what?"

"Helped her parents around the farm...cared for them through the end of their days."

"More trauma piled on her, I imagine."

"Yes, and when it was over, she was sitting out there on the farm all alone with no family support. The irony is she was left with a farm rather than a child to look after, not exactly what she had in mind."

"Something tells me you stepped in to help, Pastor."

He stirred in his chair, uneasy with the raising of his role.

"Actually, my wife lent a greater hand than I," he said. "There were few days when she didn't make a point of dropping in on her to make sure her basic needs were being met. Still, the likelihood of Charlene keeping the farm afloat was always in doubt. Eventually, she came to realize she didn't have the necessary support to continue on, so she decided to sell the property."

"At a profit, may I ask?"

"A small one—enough for her to pay off some long overdue bills."

"Then what?"

"Then we became her surrogate family. At our insistence she moved in with us and became the child we never had. It might not have been the life she wanted, but it was the only one available to her at the time."

"Did she take up an occupation?"

"At first she considered entering college, but her enthusiasm for it was lacking. She was not the intellectually curious kind to begin with, plus her mental condition during this period seemed to drain her of any zest for life."

"No social life to speak of?"

"None, other than the occasional church gatherings. As you can guess, there is little to do in Hidden Valley in the way of social recreation. People of her age—especially single people—are few and far between in these parts. Over the years, there were a few fellows in our congregation who made polite inquiries, sometimes through me, regarding her marital status, but she would invariably decline their overtures. It was probably best for everyone she did so, since she really wasn't in a state of mind to start a relationship. I'm a little embarrassed in saying this, but according to her doctor, the symptoms of bipolar disorder involve a wide range of mood swings, including excessive highs and lows, which can lead to instances of risk-taking behavior, including sexual episodes. From what I was told, the highs often reach a euphoric stage where the victim experiences a heightened sense of sensuality and an increased sexual drive. As you might expect, this can be a major cause of concern for the guardians of a young girl, especially one as attractive as Charlene. Fortunately, she took her medicine regularly, muting any severe mood swings."

A siren wailed in the background, breaking the pastor's narrative. An emergency vehicle sped down the highway, its blare eventually fading in the distance.

"You said she started seeing a doctor not long after her return?" he asked.

"Yes, when the symptoms started. It was another reason her parents were in favor of her giving up the baby."

"So, if her sister's death contributed to her condition and she didn't start seeing the doctor till after her return, is it fair to say there was a period between her sister's death and her return when she could be described as especially vulnerable?"

"Yes, and the result of it was an unwanted pregnancy, though I must say, as her doctor reminded us, the seed of her vulnerability was planted long before her sister's death."

"What made her return to Tampa?"

"A good question. My wife and I agreed that the day undoubtedly would come when she would pick up and take off. As much as I would like to think it was because of us she stuck around for as long as she did, in truth it was her daughter."

"She was in contact with her?"'

"No, it was a closed adoption. However, she never completely severed the ties, the emotional ones in particular. Perhaps you agree with me, Mr. Fraley, when I say the parental bond is the strongest. Every parent wants the best for their child. If, for whatever reason, they are unable to offer them the best, they at least want to lay a foundation, which will benefit them the remainder of their lives. The child no longer may have been legally hers, but she continued to look out for her interests from afar, in the only ways she knew how. She was convinced somewhere down the line her daughter would seek out who her birth parents were. As a result, she became fixated on two issues: one, beginning-of-life and the other, end-of-life. The latter was related to her purchase of the cemetery plot. She decided no matter what happened to her daughter during her lifetime, she always would have the option of a permanent resting place next to her, if she so decided."

"Do you feel she was contemplating taking her own life at the time of the purchase?"

"Hard to say. Her medicine helped stabilize her but did not completely eliminate her fluctuating moods. On the one hand, she came to accept her decision to give up the baby. On the other, it left a void in her life, which was difficult to fill, especially in this town where the pursuit of happiness is doubly difficult for a young woman looking to right a past she is unable or unwilling to leave behind."

"And the beginning-of-life issue?"

The pastor managed a weak smile. "As I mentioned, I do not know who fathered her child. All she would say of him is that he once told her of all the times since the beginning of time to be living on this earth, he felt blessed it was the same time as she."

"The father said that?"

"Yes. Charlene thought it nice. She did, of course, know who fathered the child and eventually wanted her daughter to know. The problem is Ohio law requires the written consent of the father or a court ruling of paternity before a father's name can be entered on the birth certificate of a child born out of wedlock."

"The father's name was not entered?"

"No. It can be entered on the certificate of an out-of-wedlock child only if both the mother and father sign a paternity affidavit. Therefore, the father must give his consent before being named. Apparently, he didn't."

"Did she give a reason for his refusal?"

"No. I don't believe it was an issue for her at the time of the birth. It only became one later, when she decided it was in her daughter's best interest to have the name entered."

"Which option was she aiming for, a court ruling or a signed affidavit?"

"She wanted to avoid a court fight, if at all possible, so she decided to seek the father's written consent."

"She told you this?"

"In an indirect way, yes. One day she came home with a copy

of a paternity affidavit form she retrieved at the library. She left it lying on the dining room table. When my wife asked her about it, she related her intention of asking her daughter's father to sign it as documentary evidence she could present to the people at the Department of Health. On receiving it they then would issue a new birth certificate having the same appearance as one which would have been issued if a marriage had occurred prior to the birth of the child."

"At what point was she considering this?"

"Right before she moved back to Tampa."

"This was the reason for her moving back? Why couldn't she have tried to get a signature without going through the trouble of moving?"

"You must remember, Mr. Fraley, Charlene was mentally impaired. Trying to apply a rationale to her behavior was a difficult exercise in many instances, as her doctor frequently advised us. He said she easily could become a prisoner of her own mind, unable to escape to the world of reality."

For an instant he considered asking for the name of her doctor but realized retrieving private medical records was an even more futile exercise.

"The doctor is aware of her death, I presume."

"Of course. He was saddened like all of us."

"Did she have a doctor in Tampa that you know of?" he asked

"I doubt it. She never mentioned one."

"Did you keep in touch with her after her move?"

"There were a few calls until the sheriff notified us of her death."

"Before her death, was she still on her medicine?"

"No way for us to be certain, though she did seem to be in the same general frame of mind as she was when living here."

"Did she mention anything about getting the affidavit signed?"

"No, and as far as I'm concerned, it's the end of the story. I've probably spoken more than I should have about the situation as is," he said, reaching a hand out to roll down the top of his desk. "I'm not sure what's behind your investigation, but wherever it leads you and whatever it uncovers, I hope you keep in mind Charlene was not living life on a level playing field, if I can borrow an old sports cliché. She made a mistake and was trying mightily to right it. Unfortunately, it was a child's mistake with adult consequences. After all, absent the proper help, she easily could become a child in mind if not body, confined there either by a mental affliction or else a determined demon."

"Let me ask you pastor, would you say she fit the description of a consenting adult?"

"I'll repeat. It was a child's mistake with adult consequences."

Adam bid the reverend farewell, leaving him once again alone with his thoughts. Before departing the church grounds, he took a final stroll up to Charlene's gravesite to pay his respects, sure of only one thing, her entire story had yet to be told.

*

"Which way to Ohio College?" he asked the shaggy-haired youngster pumping gas into his truck.

"Seventy-five miles west of here or fifty miles on past the interstate," he said, pointing a finger up the road Adam came in on. "You'll see the sign about five miles before you hit Perryville."

It was early afternoon and Adam still had time to swing by the college, if for no other reason than to turn over another stone.

An hour later he eyed the sign, a large marble marker anchored at the entrance of the main access road. A half-mile into it, a cluster of stone buildings flanked by newer red-brick structures, all set on a lush green landscape, came into view. Lodged between the buildings were courtyards ringed by flowerbeds. Several students were lounging alone on the open grass, kept company by fluffy orange squirrels flitting between stands of leafy trees. Off to the side, at the edge of a wooded area, was an athletic field occupied by a group of students engaged in a spirited soccer match. Running along the far side of the field were aluminum bleachers sprinkled with spectators, their shouts of encouragement echoing across the campus.

He followed a series of hanging signs, one of which pointed to the library building where he found a visitors' parking slot. From there he hoofed it down a pedestrian pathway leading to one of the red brick structures housing the library. Inside, a scattering of students sat in various states of studious repose at large oak tables located in the main reading room while others browsed the adjacent stacks.

He wasted no time requesting, from a librarian, school yearbooks from the mid-seventies. Minutes later he had them lined up on an empty table, four embossed lavender and gold volumes with the title *The Lancer* lettered across the top. As expected he found the class photos of both Monte Wheeler and Carlene Gibbs. Judging by their entries, they were active students, Wheeler having been named to the honor roll for all four years while also serving as co-captain of the Ohio College Lancer football squad his senior year. Carlene at one time or another was a member of the German Club, Student Senate, Pep Squad, and Student-Faculty Liaison Committee. All else was the usual happy-days stuff—photos of homecoming games, dances, festivals, reunions, and parades, enough to momentarily distract him from his present mission.

On returning the yearbooks to the librarian, he inquired about back issues of the local paper, the *Perryville Sun*, displayed on a nearby newspaper rack. He was informed it was a weekly and was available on microfilm. He requested film covering the years 1975-78, which turned out to be two reels' worth. Directed by the librarian to an alcove containing four microfilm machines, he settled in at one of the stations. Rather than scan the entire two reels, he decided to narrow his search down to the months school was in session. Working back from 1978, he launched into his search, skimming local headlines in rapid order. He discovered quickly Wheeler was a mainstay of the football squad, his performances helping the team to a conference title in his senior year. According to one article, it culminated in his being named Conference Player of the Year. Spinning through the 1977 reel and seeing much the same, his attention suddenly was grabbed by a small headline at the bottom of a September sports page.

Lancer Player Reinstated

All-conference tight end Monte Wheeler has rejoined the Ohio College Lancer football squad after a short absence, coach Jimmy Wellborn said yesterday. It was announced earlier in the day by school administrators Wheeler would be readmitted to school following the dismissal of an assault charge against him. Wellborn welcomed the player back to the squad, saying the team and player had put the episode behind them.

His interest piqued, he straightened himself in the chair and spun the reel in reverse, nearly dislodging the film from its track. The screeching drew a disgruntled look from a student trying to concentrate at the station next to him. Obviously, there was an earlier story he missed. Slowly, he again scanned the paper from the beginning of September. The second week into it, he spotted the original story at the bottom of the front page.

Lancer Player Arrested

Ohio College football player Monte Wheeler was arrested and released Saturday night following an incident in the parking lot of the Hilltop Inn, the sheriff's office said. An altercation between Wheeler and an unidentified woman led to his arrest on an assault charge. School officials said Wheeler would be placed on suspension until an investigation into the incident is completed.

He scanned carefully the three weeks between the original story and the follow-up one announcing Wheeler's reinstatement. Nothing in the interim regarding the incident appeared.

He returned the reels, asking the librarian for directions to the nearest sheriff's station. Another two miles toward town, he was told. Moments later he was back on the highway, passing the Hilltop Inn on the way. As rural taverns go, it was about as generic as could be, a maroon stucco structure with a rooftop sign bearing

112

the establishment's moniker and blue neon sign in the window promising good food and cold beer inside. A half-mile further he came upon the sheriff's station, a maize-tinted modular structure located on the outskirts of town. A reed-thin blonde female clerk with the look of someone desiring attention sat on a stool behind the service desk.

"Ma'am, I have a bit of a strange request," he said, leaning his hands against the counter. "I would like to get a copy of a sheriff's report regarding an incident at the Hilltop Inn on September 28, 1977."

The woman looked at him puzzle-eyed. "Not strange at all," she replied. "At least you have a specific date. Most people who come in here looking for past reports have no idea of the year, much less the day. Still, it's going to take a few minutes to look it up, if you'd like to have a seat over there."

He sat down on the black leather bench she had motioned to across the tiny lobby to await the retrieval of the report, paying half attention to the crackle of radio messages playing in the background as troopers called in their locations to the dispatcher.

Not long after her disappearance, the woman reappeared at the window. "Here you go," she said, waving a copy of the document in her hand.

He paid the two-buck charge for the copy and returned to the bench to review it. In bare detail the report related the series of events that transpired when troopers were called to the scene of a reported altercation at the Hilltop Inn parking lot. Upon arrival a witness informed them a man had struck a woman during the course of a heated argument, knocking her to the ground. The witness said he immediately called the sheriff's department to report the assault. The witness and another couple who arrived on the scene then helped the woman to her feet and attempted to calm the couple down until the deputies arrived. Based on the accounts of the witnesses, the man was taken into custody. He was identified as Monte Wheeler, a student at Ohio College and a resident at the school. The woman was identified as Carlene Gibbs, also a student and resident at the college.

He noted the primary witness's name—Steve Sealy—and stepped back up to the counter to ask the clerk if by chance she knew the guy.

The woman thought a moment, staring hard at the document. "There's a Steve Sealy who runs an auto garage a little farther down the road," she said. "I've only lived here five years so I can't swear it's the same guy, though." She turned to snatch a phone book from the top of a desk and leafed through it. "Yeah, he's the only Sealy in town."

Adam thanked the woman and resumed his trip toward town, spotting a "Steve's Garage" sign posted alongside the roadway less than a half-mile from the sheriff's station. It was a two-car garage fronted by a gravel parking lot. Lined up on one side of the building, next to a vending machine, were racks of used tires. At the entrance to one of the garage doors, a black-coated German Shepherd rested on all fours, his snout on the ground, his eyes tracking his approach. Inside the garage a guy working beneath a late model sedan was crawling out from beneath the car, having noticed Adam's arrival. Rising to his feet, the man tossed a grease rag onto a workbench and wiped his hands against the sides of his overalls. "Yes sir, what can I do for you?" he asked. His pleasant demeanor was at odds with his gruff exterior, featuring a pockmarked face and straw hair hanging to the base of his neck.

"I was just down at the sheriff's station looking into an old incident that occurred at the Hilltop Inn about ten years ago," he said, hands on hips. "The official report has you listed as a witness."

The man's eyes reflected surprise. "Oh yeah?"

"It had to do with an altercation or fight between a young man and woman in the parking lot...college students."

"Oh yeah, I recall it. Never saw anything like it before and hope to never see anything like it again. But why is it coming up now?"

"I'm a private investigator from Tampa, Florida. The case I'm working on involves the two people in the fight."

"But not the same case."

"Right...a more recent one. I was checking into the backgrounds of the two individuals when I happened upon this earlier incident. I was hoping you could fill me in on some of the details of the Hilltop Inn case. The sheriff's report is skimpy to say the least."

Sealy hunched his shoulders. "There really isn't much to report. I remember it being a Saturday night. I got a call at home from a buddy of mine who was out partying at the place. It's mainly a college hangout and he liked going there so he could flirt and dance with the coeds. Anyway, after leaving the place, he discovered his truck had stalled and he couldn't get it started. Said his battery was dead. So, I went over to give him a jump. When I did, he took off. Just as I was about to leave I heard this commotion on the other side of the lot. I looked over and saw this guy barking into the face of a girl. No sooner had I seen them than the guy raised his forearm and struck her a blow along the side of the head, knocking her flat to the ground." Sealy paused to shake his head. "Believe me, it was an ugly scene. He might as well have hit her with a baseball bat. Thankfully, I had a car phone in my truck I use for business so I immediately called the sheriff's office to report what happened. I then ran over to intervene, helping the gal to her feet. About the same time, another young couple came out of the bar, saw what was going on, and ran over to us. Turns out they knew the feuding couple from school. They tried to comfort the girl as best they could. Meanwhile, this guy was still acting like the school bully, pretending it was none of my business. For a moment I thought we were going to come to blows. Before we did, however, the sheriff's deputies arrived. Good thing too, because the guy had a solid build on him and I didn't have Cranky here with me," he said, motioning to his dog who had fallen asleep.

"You weren't around for the arrest?" he asked.

"Nah, I gave my statement to them and took off. Don't mind saying I was a little annoyed, because right about the time the deputies arrived, the boyfriend dropped his bullying act and went into his 'I'm sorry' routine. I don't think the deputies were buying it, though."

"How seriously was the girl injured?"

"She kept insisting she was fine and refused medical attention. She did take one hell of a blow, however. It wasn't a push or a shove, I can tell you that. It was a forearm backhand," he said, raising his and whipping it around to illustrate how it was delivered.

"It's what batterers do," Adam offered, recalling lessons from his Air Force training days. "They strike with a backhand against the side of the head. It's less likely to result in visible bruises or cuts. Did she have long hair?"

"Yes, she did."

"Better to conceal a bruise," he said. "The experienced batterers know better than to punch a woman in the face and leave evidence for everyone to see."

"Can I ask what the case you are currently working on now has to do with them?"

"Family matters," he replied.

"Yeah, those can get real nasty," he said, smiling and shaking his head as though he spoke from experience.

Adam thanked the man, hopped into his pickup, and swung it back onto the highway, kicking up a spray of pebbles. Passing the Hilltop Inn, he noticed several cars filled with energized youth converging in the parking lot. The neon sign in the tavern's window was lit bright, signaling the opening of a rocking good night for revelers. It was a sight probably not much different from one seen by passersby ten years past, one that dramatized a simple truth. A man's past was catching up with him, and who better than he to lend it a helping hand?

*

"Okay Adam, we need to talk," Peterson snapped, bursting through the office front door and making a beeline for the desk. He watched his boss's movement across the floor with a mixture of surprise and concern, scrambling his memory to recall a time he had seen the guy in such an agitated state. After all, he was the man who had experienced it all on the job, the one least likely to become unhinged by the news of the day.

"What's up?" he asked, attempting to reset a normal tone.

"Got a call from Stan Maroney, brother of Rita Gordon, in case you forgot," he said, flopping his briefcase on the desk and dragging up a chair.

"More in-law problems?" he asked.

"Wish it were," he said, snatching a water bottle from his briefcase and taking a quick swig. "Apparently, law enforcement officials are getting feedback from the front lines regarding our investigations into the bridge jumping incident and are becoming perturbed about it, to put it mildly."

"Perturbed about what?'

"About us acting like they didn't do their job, or worse, covering it up."

"What do they plan on doing about it?"

"They've already done something. Tomorrow morning we are scheduled to meet with the Chief Deputy Sheriff at nine o'clock at the Sheriff's Office Annex over on Bay Street."

"The Chief Deputy Sheriff?"

"The second-in-command himself...Stan Conley. How do you like them apples?"

"Stan Conley?"

"Yeah, you know him?"

"In another life."

"One life at a time, Adam. Let's stick to this one for now."

Peterson washed down another mouthful from his bottle and took a deep breath.

"So, what do you make of it?" Adam asked.

"Make of the meeting?"

"Yes."

"All Maroney would say is it concerned the bridge incident, nothing more. If I had to guess, I would say we were in for a scolding, maybe more."

He took quick measure of the revelation and the worried man across from him. "Look, Pete, this is all my doing. Why do you need to be there?"

"Because your name is attached to mine. Secondly, I'm expected to be, according to Maroney. Thirdly, I want to be."

Peterson screwed the cap back on his water bottle and shoved it into his briefcase.

"I'll confess to my concern over your getting involved, Adam, though I admit it comes belatedly. As I've said, it's important to maintain good relations with law enforcement agencies. God forbid you uncover something they failed to uncover. The fact is they can make or break an operation like ours. One bad word from them to the media or whomever and you've got a stain no amount of public relations is going to remove."

"Considering the amount of time you've been in the business and had dealings with them, they're not going to cut you some slack?"

"Not if it's big toes getting stepped on," he said.

"Like Wheeler's? He's no law enforcement official."

"Make no mistake about it, Adam. He's part of the establishment. Part of the price of membership in it is to look out for each other's back. It's their safety net in case one of the pilings breaks."

"So what is there to do to prepare for tomorrow?" he asked, aware the stakes were much higher with his boss having been dragged into the line of fire. "Do you know the Chief Deputy?"

"Personally…no. I've met him on a couple of occasions and he seemed a reasonable guy. However, all he would have to do to make things really sticky for us is to bring his boss along or boss's niece for that matter. Wouldn't that be a trip? I can tell you this, the less said by us, the better. The ball is in their court. Let's see what they do with it."

"You're saying we avoid getting into the details of the case?"

"Not unless he drags us there. I'm not sure we could tell him much more than he already knows."

"Including the fact that Charlene Gibbs had a child?"

"Speculation on our part."

"Speculation no longer. I learned over the weekend she in fact had one."

Peterson tossed him a quizzical look. "Oh, yeah?"

"I took another quick trip to Hidden Valley to speak with her pastor. He confirmed our suspicions."

"Where's the kid?"

"She gave her up for adoption."

"Wheeler the father?"

"She never said and the pastor doesn't know."

"No matter. Tomorrow morning we don't volunteer anything."

Adam mentioned his side trip to Perryville and the parking lot incident, asking his boss what he made of it.

"It doesn't register on the radar screen, then or now, except maybe in Perryville. Once the charges are dropped, the system spits it out and goes on to the next case," he said, flipping his fingers up and down in a dismissive gesture.

"Can't say I was surprised at the report," Adam said, putting more weight to it.

"You know how it goes with those guys, Adam. They're charming when they are not battering."

"Still, it stands as supportive evidence," he said, unwilling to let it go.

"For what? That he's a smart ass? The guy was on the honor roll and a batterer. I'd say he fits the definition of one perfectly."

"It makes you wonder what other incidents might be on his record."

"Like you said, he's probably become experienced enough at it to avoid detection."

"Do you suppose the sheriff did any prior checking on his niece's husband-to-be?"

"Even hard-nosed sheriffs like Ward Fletcher sometimes assume the best in people, especially if it is someone with the stature of Wheeler. A good catch for the niece, the family was undoubtedly thinking."

From his detached tone, it was clear the Perryville revelation mattered little to his boss whose mind was occupied with the upcoming meeting with the Chief Deputy. In going on the offense they suddenly found themselves playing defense.

"There's one other angle to the story I still don't quite get, Pete," he said, switching focus. "Wheeler and Charlene were headed north on the bridge. Why?" he asked, throwing out his hands. "There's nothing south of the Skyway worth seeing until you hit Bradenton. Plus, he rented the car for only two days."

Peterson settled back in his chair, his early agitation replaced by resignation.

"Could have been for any number of reasons, including the seven-year itch, if I got my years straight. He hadn't seen her since 1980, right?"

"As far as we know."

"So he's already tired of the Sheriff's niece and back comes the black-haired beauty into his life. You think a guy like him is going to pass her up given his track record?"

"You haven't got a rent-a-room routine to go with your rent-a-car one, have you?"

"You're thinking he may have stopped for some afternoon delight?"

"Possibility."

"Slim one, and what if he did? It's not criminal activity we're talking about," Peterson said.

"It puts him on the bridge."

"We already know that and I wouldn't be surprised if the Chief Deputy Sheriff knows it."

"The question is whether Wheeler's father-in-law knows it," he said. "Maybe, and my point is what if he does? It still doesn't amount to a crime."

"What about the withholding of evidence?"

"I repeat, evidence of what?" his boss said. "Remember, Adam, your gal Charlene was not exactly running around with a halo propped over her head during all of this."

The reality of Peterson's observation was not lost on him. "I learned in Hidden Valley she had it in mind for the father of the child to sign an affidavit admitting his paternity. She even went to the trouble of obtaining the form and planned on bringing it back to Tampa with her, undoubtedly to get his signature."

"Okay, she's carrying a blank affidavit. Say it's even signed. Where is it and what good is it going to do you even if it does turn up?"

"She had a handbag with her when she jumped," he said, attempting to hang his hat onto something, anything, even if by a thread.

"Okay, she had a handbag with her," Peterson said condescendingly. "All women do. Like I said, the ball is in their court."

*

They walked to the sheriff's office annex a few blocks from their office, joining the early morning flow of pedestrians quick-stepping it to their respective workplaces. In an earlier life, the building served as a vocational-technical school. Later, it was taken over and refurbished by the county to relieve overcrowding at the sheriff's office headquarters a half-mile away. Entering the gray stone structure, they were greeted by a desk clerk and escorted down a brightly lit cream-colored corridor to a conference room filled with the standard bland government furnishings. A brawny man dressed in a tan uniform sat stiffly at an egg-shaped plastic table awaiting their arrival. The instant Adam eyed him he realized the Stan Conley of his other life and current life were one and the same. Sitting next to him, and looking every bit as rigid, was Monte Wheeler. "Have a seat, fellows," Conley said, motioning to two metal chairs backed up against a wall. As they dragged the chairs screeching across the floor to the table, the chief deputy rose and ambled to the door, closing off the sound of the desk clerk's footsteps fading down the hallway. Returning to his chair, he flipped open a large maroon notebook lying on the table. Before launching into the business at hand, however, he casually turned to Adam, and in an aside overheard by all, asked "How's the discharge appeal coming along?"

"Fine," he replied in the same curt vein he did to his father.

"I've been asked to submit an opinion on the case. Shouldn't be too long before a decision is reached."

In his other life, Conley was an Air Force Reserve Officer, one of many who rotated in and out of active duty at MacDill Air Force Base. On a number of occasions, Adam would notice him sitting at his desk at the personnel office where he was assigned, which explained his being asked to submit an opinion regarding his case.

The chief deputy ran a hand through his thinning brown hair, and eyed those about him before landing his hard look on Peterson. "Pete, this here is Monte Wheeler," he said, nodding to his left side. "Mr. Wheeler and Mr. Fraley…I believe you two have met."

To his relief the introductions were accomplished without the need of handshakes, anemic nods sufficing. He was sure his boss at first was as surprised as he by Wheeler's presence, though he gave no indication of it. There was no mistaking the message being sent them, however. The law was on the editor's side. Whether you're involved in a traffic ticket case, murder investigation, or anything in-between, it's comforting to have a person in uniform sitting at your right-hand side, especially if he's bearing the insignia of a chief deputy.

Once everyone was settled into their seats, Conley reached into his briefcase and pulled out a recorder, positioning it in the middle of the table. "I don't think anyone will have any objection to having this session on the record, right?"

Conley looked directly at Peterson for a reaction, knowing full well Peterson spoke for both of them. For a moment his boss hesitated and then shrugged, prompting the chief deputy to punch the record button and commence with his opening monologue.

"It has been brought to my attention by several sources, Pete, that your business has been conducting an investigation into the Charlene Gibbs suicide incident, a case the department closed on some time back. Mr. Wheeler, in particular, is concerned about your actions, since the incident involved members of his family in a tragedy he legitimately believed had been put to rest. Given the findings, my question is a simple one. Is there anything leading you to believe the incident was something other than what was reported by the investigating officers?"

Conley looked across the table, his eyes darting between the two of them. Meanwhile, Wheeler was avoiding eye contact as artfully as a homecoming queen in a classroom full of nerds, staring over their shoulders at the wall behind them with a blank expression on his face.

"Nothing to contradict the official report," Peterson said matter-of-factly.

Conley stretched his back in his chair, as though a balky nerve or cramp was preventing him from sitting comfortably.

"Why then are you pursuing this case, if I may ask?"

Adam could not sit by and let his boss take the heat for something he was primarily responsible for, despite the pre-meeting strategy he agreed upon.

"It was my idea," he said, drawing Wheeler's attention away from the wall. "I was curious as to some of the details, since I was a witness to the event."

"As a witness, did you not report everything you saw to the investigating officer?"

"I did."

"So what made you curious?"

"As Mr. Wheeler may have told you, the fact her sister was killed on the original Skyway led to some questions on my part."

"In what regard?" Conley asked.

"The failure of the media to mention the sister connection, for one thing."

"And as anyone who has any knowledge of how the media works knows, Mr. Fraley, suicides are treated differently out of respect to the families," Wheeler snapped, ending his silence.

"What other questions?" Conley asked, moving things right along.

"She had a handbag with her. Was it recovered?" he asked, recalling it clutched in her hands.

"There was no handbag recovered, according to the marine patrol people. Why do you ask?"

"Curious," he responded, glancing at Wheeler whose eyes again were fixed on the wall, as if lowering them to their level meant lowering himself.

"Anything else you are curious about?"

"Yes. How did she make it to the bridge in the first place?" he asked, mindful he was treading close to the edge of confrontation.

"We don't know," Conley replied. "We reviewed the bridge tapes just like you reviewed the bridge tapes and discovered what you no doubt discovered, a lot of bad camera angles."

The eight-hundred-pound gorilla suddenly appearing in the room came in the form of a follow-up question, a giant inference dangling out there for the asking. *Did Mr. Wheeler provide the ride for Miss Gibbs?*

He looked to his boss, sitting poker-faced with hands in lap and eyes adrift for some sort of signal to pull the trigger on the loaded question, a subtle okay to risk the farm, but none was forthcoming.

"Would we have liked to have discovered how she arrived on the bridge? Sure, but it certainly wasn't a critical factor for us in determining the cause of death," the chief deputy said. "After all, Mr. Fraley, you were the prime witness to the incident, the one who described to the on-site investigating officer the series of events as you witnessed them. And for your information, no one else subsequently contacted us claiming to be a witness to the incident."

Conley glanced at his notebook before continuing. "You were asked at the end of the interview if there was anything else you witnessed not covered in the questioning and your response was no. You also were asked if you had any idea how the woman arrived on the bridge and your answer was no," he said, closing his notebook. "This was deemed a suicide, Mr. Fraley, based to a great degree on input from you. I must admit I find it puzzling to know what subsequently got into you to pursue this matter further."

Wheeler straightened himself in his chair, unable to contain himself. "I can tell you what got into him," he scoffed, lowering his eyes to the assembled. "Charlene Gibbs is what got into him. As Mr. Fraley discovered that night, my sister-in-law was an exceptionally beautiful woman, so he decided to indulge himself. Never mind the fact she was in an extremely vulnerable mental state. He had her attention, by default of course. And look at the result. Go home and take a look in the mirror, Mr. Fraley. The truth is, under any other circumstances, my sister-in-law would not have given you a second look, much less a first one."

"Bite me, Wheeler," his boss barked, roused from his placid state.

"Okay, okay, fellows, enough of this," Conley broke in. "Let's not allow personal feelings to cloud our judgment. The purpose of this meeting is to clear the air regarding a closed investigation. According to the official report, there was no criminal activity involved in the incident. I take it everyone here is in agreement with this finding. If not, now is the time to state your case."

Conley eyed the two of them from across the table. Each held his tongue, a tacit admission to Conley's claim.

"Good. I trust this will end the matter then," he said, pressing the off button on the recorder. He slipped the machine into his briefcase and rose to leave, beating Peterson to the door. Wheeler followed, pausing on his way to lean and whisper in his ear. "Why don't you just settle for imagining what great stuff she was," he said, his lips quirking at the corners.

"What was that all about?" his boss asked, having observed the incident from the doorway.

"A confession of sorts," he said. "And he didn't even stick around for his penance and absolution."

*

A silence settled over them on their walk back, sticking to them like the sultry air blowing in off the gulf waters. What was there to say? They in effect signed off on the official investigation, no doubt the very purpose of the meeting. Victor Gantt could not have done any better in getting a client to sign off on a shady insurance settlement before a lawyer busted in to derail the agreement.

"And what the hell was that little chitchat over a discharge appeal all about?" Pete asked, breaking the silence. "You didn't receive an honorable one?"

"No, I didn't."

"Something you didn't tell me about, of course. I don't care for surprises, Adam, particularly when they are sprung on me in an important meeting."

"I can explain…"

"Explain later," he snapped, launching another round of silence.

*

"Sorry, Pete. I shouldn't have gotten you involved in this in the first place," he said on their arrival back at the office. "And to make matters worse, I go and ditch our game plan."

Peterson flung his briefcase on the desk. "Forget it. I shouldn't have agreed to the meeting in the first place or at least insisted on keeping it off the record," he responded in a resigned manner. "The fact is we didn't have much to throw at them in the way of hard evidence. The only solid pieces we had linking Wheeler to the bridge were the tapes and they've been erased by now. Everything else is supposition, and even if it wasn't, there's still no underlying crime involved, unless you want to call Wheeler himself a walking crime, which may not be far from the truth."

Wheeler's words from the meeting…those both bellowed and whispered, lingered with Adam the remainder of the day. Certainly, he was right about Charlene not giving him a second look under normal circumstances, yet she did give him a second one on the bridge, speaking to him in words far more meaningful than he could have understood at the time. Yes, she was vulnerable. No, he was not responsible for her final act. Yes, he felt a personal obligation to her, though he could not explain why. And yes, he was determined to level the playing field that her pastor had pointed out she was playing on, so justice in some form could be served. After much thought, Adam came to recognize his problem as an indigenous one. *He* was playing on the wrong field.

CHAPTER EIGHT

The first time Adam laid eyes on Nancy Egan she was standing tall in front of his journalism class in her smart cream-colored suit with pointer in hand. The vision reminded him of a female captain who once strolled the head of a classroom during an Air Force security course he was assigned to take. Everything about her was neat and orderly from her proper dress and close-cut tawny hair, to her clear facial features and confident manner. He guessed her to be in her mid-thirties, though he would be the first to admit he was a bad guesser all around when it came to women. A brief bio included in a class handout indicated she had enough years behind her to compile an impressive resume and currently was in her second year of serving as an adjunct professor. Of greater interest to him was her full-time job as Managing Editor of the *West Florida Gazette*, the only daily newspaper in the region still considered a competitor to the *Bay Area Beacon*. The idea of bringing the bridge incident issue to her attention had percolated in the back of his mind long enough. It was time to seek out her opinion. The opportunity arrived with her latest class assignment, an essay in which they were to posit an ethical dilemma for a fledgling journalist.

"For those of you who may have trouble coming up with a suitable topic, I will be available for consultation one-hour prior to our next class," she announced to them in her precise fashion. No trouble at all he wanted to shout out in appreciation, but rather than wait around for the next session to garner an opinion, he played the laggard after the close of class, approaching her as she shuffled together her lecture notes at the head table.

"Excuse me, professor Egan, I was wondering if I could get a head start on the essay assignment and run my proposed topic by you now?" he asked from a polite distance.

"You've already settled on one?" she asked, raising her light green eyes to him.

"Yes, it's an issue I'm currently facing in my job," he said, spontaneously reaching out to slide a front row chair in front of her desk and settling into it.

"You're a journalist?" she asked in surprise.

"No, I'm a private investigator, a novice one. However, my dilemma involves the newspaper profession in a major way."

She stuffed her notes into her briefcase and set it aside. "Well then, let me hear it."

He related everything, from the instant he spotted Charlene on the bridge to the moment he and his boss walked out of their meeting with Wheeler and the Chief Deputy.

All the while, she patiently listened with arms crossed on her lap, her eyes never leaving his. When he finished she uncrossed her arms and crossed her legs, grabbing one at the knee below the hemline with both hands. He knew he had her hooked. How could she not be? He was talking about her major competitor.

She paused before responding, as if to completely absorb his narrative. "Who in this story is faced with an ethical dilemma?" she finally asked, throwing him off balance. After all, he wasn't expecting an immediate oral test on it.

"Me, for one."

"In what way?"

"To report or not report the entire story."

"To whom?"

"To the authorities…to you…to somebody…I don't know."

"You're looking at the story from the perspective of a private investigator, Mr. Fraley. It seems to me it does not pose an ethical dilemma as much as it does a legal one in your situation. If, on the other hand, a journalist becomes privy to the same body of information, would he feel duty-bound to include it in a story if it flew against the newspaper's official or unofficial policy?"

"Or the objections of a boss," he interjected. "I could present it from the perspective of a new hire working under a guy like Wheeler."

"There you go," she said, tossing out her hands. "It opens up all sorts of ethical questions for the boss and subordinate."

"Do you know Wheeler?" he asked offhandedly.

"On a professional basis," she said. "Why do you ask?"

"Because I would like a professional's opinion of this story, or non-story."

"As a professor, I would say it poses interesting issues. As an editor, I would say it raises ticklish issues. In case you are not aware, we also covered the story at the *Gazette*. If I recall right, our piece was similar in substance to the *Beacon's*. What you tell me puts a whole new perspective on it, however."

"I'm sure your reporter was limited to the same information by the authorities, so it comes as no surprise."

"Could be. I'll have to check with him to find out for sure," she said.

The lights in the classroom suddenly blinked on and off, a not-so-subtle message from the maintenance crew milling about in the hallway it was time to clear the room.

"I'll let you know what I come up with," she said, as they parted ways out the door.

He left with a sense of satisfaction. He had dangled the story in front of her and she bit on it as expected. Whether she now would run with it or spit it out was another matter. One way or the other, the life of the story was hanging by a thread.

*

It may not have risen to the level of post-traumatic syndrome, but each believed they let the other down, Adam for dragging his boss into a questionable case to begin with, Peterson for bending to the will of the chief deputy. All things considered, it was Peterson who had the most on the line. He and his wife spent nearly a lifetime building a small business into a solvent operation, one that provided them the opportunity to spend the remainder of their lives living out a dream in the Keys. No, it was not the time for him to be making the kind of mistakes capable of crumbling the couple's castle in the sky. Adam, on the other hand, had the time to not only recover but also learn from a rookie's errors. He therefore decided to temporarily take himself out of the surveillance game, asking his boss if he could concentrate on office duties for the time being until he had a better handle on the business. Peterson readily agreed, saying in so many words it was what he had expected of Adam in the first place.

So, back to the basics he went, compiling reports, handling phone calls, maintaining records, researching computer files and conducting routine background checks for prior arrests, convictions, and civil judgments. All necessary work, yet hardly the adrenalin-inducing activities and atmospherics associated with working the street. The private investigator's preventative medicine is how Peterson described the work. Something as simple as making sure there were no conflicts of interest at play was critical to the operation. Nothing more deflating or embarrassing than learning halfway through a case you were piling up points for both sides. Even worse was for competing clients to become aware of it. Yes, both the routine and the risky were required in the search for the truth. The question was what to do with it once you finally had it in hand, for in the end, the truth was that the *truth* was not always on your client's side.

*

"What page did she say we were on?" Eva Green asked, landing her cool hand on his forearm.

"One-seventy-five," he replied without so much as a glance.

Every class seemed to have one—the student who paid more attention to classmates than the professor. With her penchant for rubbernecking during lectures and table-hopping during breaks, Eva easily qualified as the class social butterfly. By now her overtures to him were as predictable as Tampa's late afternoon thunderstorms. Early on he decided to keep his responses and gestures to the minimum, like the young misses he read about touring the fountains of Rome who minded their manners, lest they inadvertently send a message to prowling males they might later regret. In the beginning, he was flattered by the attention, but the last thing he needed at the moment was for her apparent interest in him to rise above a distraction. Not that she was lacking attractions.

It was more a matter of her concealing them with her preference for colorless stirrup slacks and matching bland blouses. Get out of the stirrups and into some jeans and heels, he was tempted to tell her. Nonetheless, once past the wardrobe, a friendly face framed by short jet-black hair was there to greet you. At any moment, her hazel eyes and thin mouth looked ready to break into a smile at the least prompting. And besides, who was he to be scoring beauty points? Ask the executive editor of the *Bay Area Beacon* that question.

"Thanks," she said, leafing her text to the correct page.

Halfway through the semester, professor Egan, in an exercise he would never forgive her for, asked members of the class to jot down on a piece of paper the one word that best described the person sitting next to them. They were then to exchange the notes. At the end of the semester, the exercise would be repeated, the professor assured them, the point of it being to illustrate how one's view of another can change dramatically over a short span of time.

Enthusiastic is how he described his tablemate, bringing a smile to her face. *Serious* she wrote in return, followed by multiple exclamation marks, forcing from him the semblance of a smile. Presently, they were only a few classes away from a repeat of the exercise, though he was convinced neither he nor she likely would stray from their original observations.

"Mr. Fraley," I would like to see you after class," the teacher said over the chatter of classmates at the end of her lecture.

He waited until the other students packed their backpacks and were fleeing out the door before approaching her desk.

"I wanted to let you know…"

The overhead lights flickered on and off, signaling the maintenance crew's impatience. Apparently, the rules required the room to be vacated by a certain time, for she offered no objection.

"It appears they want us out already," she said, lifting her briefcase to her lap while contemplating the situation. "How about continuing this over at Breakers?"

"The coffee shop?"

"Yes. Do you know where it is?"

"Sure. I pass by it nearly every day on the way home," he said, pumped by the prospect of engaging his teacher in conversation in a private setting.

Cuddled on a corner between an ice cream shop and a deli, Breakers attracted an eclectic mix of customers, ranging from young professional types to neighborhood folk. Easily recognizable by its yellow-brick exterior, it sported a green and white-striped awning stretching the length of its exterior. Inside, clusters of dark leather couches, small wooden tables and chairs, and low-level bookcases competed for space on a caramel-colored tile floor. Interspersed among the furnishings were terracotta planters sprouting fleshy-leaved red geraniums, while overhead, ceiling fans rotated in silence between rows of dim track lighting.

He was the first to arrive, taking a minute to observe the framed cartoon caricatures of famed intellectuals, from Einstein to

Schweitzer, lining the walls. Moments later, his teacher arrived, at which point they stepped to the service counter to order two decafs, before settling in at a corner table.

"Busy place for a weeknight," she said above the folk-rock sounds piping low in the background.

She wore a burgundy suit with a collared yellow blouse, a combination befitting her professional image. It contrasted sharply with Adam's casual wear, a preference he attributed to his rural roots. Somewhere down the career path it was likely to become an issue and admittedly a legitimate one.

"I wanted to get back with you regarding the bridge incident," she said. "I spoke on the phone to the reporter who was assigned to the story. He happens to be out of town at the moment working on another assignment. He informed me he relied heavily on the sheriff's report. He also checked the coroner's findings, which contained nothing to contradict the sheriff's account. It did indicate there were no drugs present in her system at the time of death. He considered contacting you but was told by authorities everything you had to say was in the official report. Perhaps he was mistaken."

"No, he would have gotten nothing more from me at the time," he said. "Was there anything else he came up with?"

"He said he had a folder full of case notes and would turn it over to me when he returned."

"Are you interested in this as a news story, Miss Egan?" he asked expectantly, observing her ringless fingers wrapped around her coffee cup.

She took a sip of the brew. "Yes, it has potential."

"Newspaper potential?"

"Editors generally look at stories with two questions in mind. Is it information owed to the public and/or is it information of interest to the public? These are issues we struggle with every day. Definitely, it meets the latter criteria. The other question we usually end up asking is whether there is any good reason not to run with the story."

"Is there any reason not to?"

"Was this your interest in bringing the story to my attention, Mr. Fraley? Were you seeking an alternate outlet for it?"

"I'd be lying if I said it didn't cross my mind."

She shifted in her chair, crossed her legs, and smoothed her dress to the knee. "I mentioned I knew Monte Wheeler only on a professional basis. The one occasion I did come face-to-face with him was at a job interview. It so happened that when he was promoted from city editor to executive editor, his former post came open. I was the features editor for our paper at the time and decided to apply for the position, feeling it represented an opportunity to advance my career. Anyway, I was among those invited for an interview. I learned long ago a job interview not only provides an interview panel the opportunity to judge your qualifications, it also gives the applicant the chance to measure the merits of the prospective employer. It turned out Monte Wheeler was on the panel and its prime player. As far as job interviews go, it was typical fare, until we got down to the final question, which struck me as quite unprofessional."

He furrowed his brow, inviting an explanation.

"It's not unusual for the closing question of an interview to be a toot-your-own-horn one, something along the lines of 'Is there anything else we should know about you, something we haven't asked that you feel might help you in being hired for this position?"

She took another sip of coffee, slid her cup aside, clasped her hands on the table, and looked him in the eye. "Instead, he asked me if I had any skeletons in my closet."

"Well, do you?" he asked in jest.

"None that would interest you," she said through her first smile of the evening. "Which is exactly what I told him. I left feeling the exchange was a deal breaker. Three days later I received a call from his secretary informing me I had been selected as one of the three finalists for the job. I told her to tell him I was going to narrow the odds for the other two candidates and withdraw my name from consideration. That was the extent of my dealings with Mr. Wheeler. Every other opinion I have of him is an educated guess."

"Can you give me one?" he asked.

"Sons of publishers come in all forms. 'Like father, like son' does not always hold true with them. At one small daily I was working at, the son of the publisher took over the reins following his father's death. He immediately turned into an absentee owner, traveling the world on the pretense he was on assignment. He sent us back lengthy articles on regional issues in places like Bangladesh, expecting us to run them as features, as if the locals cared what was going on half way around the world. In contrast to his father who took a deep interest in local matters and earned the community's respect, he hardly knew who was running for mayor from one election to the next. About twice a year he would show up at the place to make sure it was still standing. Having said that, I don't consider Mr. Wheeler to be of the same mind. Perhaps because he operates in a larger market, I see him as caught up in the power game. With all the mergers and takeovers in the publishing business, it opens up great opportunities to move up the corporate ladder. It could be he feels he is missing out on the advancements. It tends to drive up a person's intensity level when they cannot accept failure. If unavailable in the workplace, they look for conquests elsewhere to bolster their egos."

"Women included," he noted.

"Particularly if they are considered a prize," she said.

He pondered her story. "The puzzling thing about this whole matter is what Charlene Gibbs saw in the guy," he said. "I know she was vulnerable but what is there of him to like?"

"I'll take another educated guess. Most likely, he penetrated her defenses by convincing her of his love for her. Readers of *Wuthering Heights* wonder what it is that draws Catherine to

Heathcliff, despite his terrible dark side. The simple explanation is she loves him for loving her. It's a woman thing, I don't mind saying."

"Lasting from one bridge tragedy to another," he said.

"You know, someone once predicted in a letter-to-the-editor to us the collapse of the old Skyway."

"Far-sighted guy."

"He also was making hundreds of other dire predictions, none of which came true. It shows if you make enough of them, sooner or later, one is bound to come true. You then can proclaim yourself a prognosticator of the first order."

"Did you run the letter?"

"No, for many good reasons and one bad one. The person who edited the letters section was already afraid to travel the old bridge. Rather than cross it, she would take the long journey around the bay to make it to work."

A group of spirited young people spilling through the coffee shop's front entrance caught their attention. The group immediately headed for the service counter where they milled about placing and waiting for their orders to be filled. Among them was Eva Green who upon spotting them across the room raised her eyebrows and cup in recognition before returning her attention to her friends.

"How are you and Miss Green getting along?" she asked, tilting her head in expectation of his reply.

"How does it look like we are getting along?" he asked in return, hoping that would end it.

"She seems like a nice young woman, Adam."

He nodded dismissively for his attention was elsewhere. Sitting with your teacher in a setting outside the norm had a way of creating a stir, within and without. Granted, Miss Egan was more attractive than beautiful but factor in the class, the mix of mind and manners, and you easily were distracted enough to keep Charlene Gibbs off your mind.

"Back to Charlene Gibbs," she said, dousing the notion. "You believed she brought an affidavit along with her on her return to Tampa. That would indicate to me she was planning a short stay, not a permanent one."

"But she also would have signed a lease agreement at Mid-Town Apartments, which would indicate otherwise. Who knows? People with disturbed minds do disturbing things."

A roar of laughter arose from Eva Green's party gathered in a far corner. He had noticed her occasional glances directed their way, giving rise to personal unease on his part.

"How did you end up in the newspaper profession?" he asked, setting aside the distraction.

"It was hereditary. My father was a sportswriter in Chicago, my home of origin. He was forced to take early retirement because of a severe deterioration in his vision. I was still in elementary school at the time, having arrived late in my parents' marriage. Other than my mother, his other great love in life was baseball. Despite his handicap he still liked to sit in the bleachers and soak in the surroundings. I would tag along as his seeing eye and ended up learning how to fill out the score sheets, which he religiously kept prior to his retirement. Those were the days of the Go-Go Sox...Nellie Fox...Minnie Minoso...Ted Kluzewski. Ever hear of them?"

"Can't say I have."

"It was enough to spur my interest in sports, so I ended up pursuing a journalism degree in college with the idea of following in my father's footsteps. Later on he helped me land a job on the sports desk of his old newspaper. He came to regret his helping hand, however."

"Why so?"

"This was a time when the issue of female sports reporters in male locker rooms was heating up. I was taking some guff but it didn't bother me nearly as much as it did my father. At his urging I moved to the news desk. Later on, he and my mother retired here. I then began looking for a job in this area, so I could keep an eye on them. That's how I ended up with the *Gazette*."

"Too bad about the sports reporter thing," he commented.

"Yes, I enjoyed the sports beat…still do, though I'm strictly a participant now…swimming, tennis, jogging…those sorts of things, which explains my preference for outdoor activities."

And her trim figure, he thought.

"All in all, it turned out to be an okay trade by me," she said. "I once considered doing a lengthy human interest piece exploring the locker-room issue and what it represented for the profession but decided to let it pass. I felt it might come across as so many sour grapes."

He took a final swig of his coffee, while digesting her last thought.

"I'd like to propose a trade between us, Miss Egan," he said point blank.

"A trade? I hope there's not a player-to-be-named-later in what you're going to propose. It's a deal-killer," she said.

"No, a straight-up one—my Charlene Gibbs story for your locker-room one," he responded quickly.

"You forget, Mr. Fraley. They have yet to be written."

"A trade of topics then."

She slowly downed the remaining drops of her coffee, pondering the proposition.

"You're welcome to do your essay on the locker-room issue. However, I cannot commit to publishing the Gibbs story, if that's what you are proposing. There are several factors to consider first."

"But you're agreeable to the swap, right?"

She studied the tabletop for a moment, before slowly lifting her eyes to him. "Okay you've got yourself a deal."

"Now if I could only find someone to trade my Shakespeare assignment with."

"Another essay in the works? I hope your muse isn't on

vacation."

"Yeah, another essay. We're into Hamlet. The instructor wants us to quote 'do a short essay placing in context Hamlet's observation that there is no right or wrong, only thinking makes it so.' Got any ideas?"

"Am I crossing an ethical line here, offering input to a student in a colleague's class?"

"Seems alright to me. I'm just asking for an opinion, not an answer. It's sort of depressing when you think about it, the notion there is no right or wrong."

"Well, if I recall my Shakespeare right, there's the rub. Isn't Hamlet the one who wants to end his thinking so he isn't bothered by matters of right and wrong? After all, his belief system has been pulled out from under him by the manner of his father's death, so he has nothing to fall back on."

"Yeah, I'm certainly no literary expert but it always seems like the troubled individuals Shakespeare portrays are forever toeing the borderline between the light and dark sides of life, like there is a constant battle going on between their hearts and minds for control."

"What do you believe in, Adam?" she asked out of the blue, her eyes fixed on him.

"What do I believe in? You mean like in life?"

"Yes, in life."

Only in a coffee shop adjacent to a campus could a question like this come up, he mused. If they were in Shark's Lounge down the street he would be shooting both the bull and pool with her, at the same time trying to get a phone number. No way could he avoid it here, however. Plus she had a voice at once soothing and authoritative, the kind that invites attention and introspection whether in a coffee shop or a classroom.

"Is this some sort of test, Miss Egan?" he asked.

"A test of my curiosity," she said.

He took a sip of coffee, pondering the question. "Okay, I'll bite.

I believe in the wisdom of the ages," he said in mock seriousness. "How's that?'

A smile creased her face. "Can you narrow it down a bit for me, like what does the wisdom of the ages tell us about the purpose of life?"

"That's narrowing it down?"

"You strike me as a thoughtful man. It interests me to know what bits of wisdom you have accumulated thus far in your life and what they tell you about the world," she said, tweaking him with her smiling eyes.

"I have learned one thing about the purpose of life," he said, leaning half way across the table to express it. "Whatever it is, it applies as much to the guy herding goats in fourth-century Mesopotamia as it does to the two of us sitting here," he said.

She nodded, as if he accidentally hit on a point, leaving him unsure of what to think of a woman who made him think.

"Let me see if I understand you correctly. The purpose of life lies in the past and to discover it, that's where we must look," she said.

"Yes. Look to the past for your direction in life. What is it someone said…past is prologue? It works in the private investigation business as well, except a person's past more times leads to an ending rather than a beginning."

"You're thinking it's time to switch the subject."

He shrugged.

"A communications professor of mine once advanced the notion it is better to start a conversation with the big talk rather than the small talk or else you may never advance past the chit-chat stage to what he called meaningful verbal intercourse," she said.

"Sort of the way men think about foreplay," he said, wishing he hadn't.

It was enough to turn her gaze from him to the surroundings, before scooting her chair back and picking up her handbag, signaling it was time to go.

"Wait," he said, quickly raising a hand. "I have one more favor to ask of you before we leave."

She settled back into her chair, handbag in lap.

"Do you have a pen?" he asked.

"Yes," she said hesitantly.

"May I borrow it?"

She self-consciously sorted through the bag, pulled out a pen and handed it to him. "What is this all…"

"It's about something I learned in class," he said, scribbling on the back of his napkin. When finished, he returned her pen. "Now I'd like for you to jot down the one word that best describes the person sitting across from you."

For a moment she appeared reluctant to play the game, eyeing him thoughtfully. Then without further hesitation, she flipped her napkin over, scribbled on it, and slid it across the table into his view.

Observant, it read in an elegant handwriting.

In turn, he slid his napkin across to her, whereupon she casually glanced at his scribbling before smiling her final smile of the night—a half smile—a wry one.

"Time to go," she said, dropping the note into her handbag.

He followed her out, brushing past plants and people in equal measure, all the while feeling the eyes of Eva Green on his back.

"Good night, Mr. Fraley," his teacher said on parting, leaving him to wonder if sometime in the not too distant future there would be a "good night, Adam" coming from her lips.

*

"What a surprise to see you here," called the voice he cared not to hear on the heels of his professor's departure. "I've never seen you here before."

Adam stood aside his pickup, fumbling for his keys, surprised yet not surprised to see Eva Green approaching at a leisurely pace.

"Second time," he replied in a clipped tone.

"Don't you love the atmosphere in there?" she asked in a not-so-coy reference to the company he was keeping.

"Where are your friends?" he asked in return.

She shifted the weight on her feet. "They left. I told them I was going to stick around for a while and take a cab home. But then you walked by and I decided to ask you for a ride, if you don't mind."

Not the end to the evening he fancied but what choice did he have in the matter, unless he wanted to play the role of cad? "Hop in," he said, motioning to the passenger side door fronting the street.

He climbed into the pickup and reached across the front seat to unlatch the door. The moment she swung it open, a flood of blinding light filled the pickup's interior. From the corner of his eye, Adam caught the high beams of a vehicle fast approaching from the rear. Instinctively, he knew. The driver was on a collision course.

"Watch it!" he shouted to Eva, as he grabbed for her arm to pull her through the opened door and out of harm's way.

A thud of metal, a piercing scream, a blow to the head and the bright light turned to darkness.

*

The light returned the instant he opened his eyes to the blinding rays of the morning sun streaming through the windows of a hospital room. He squinted beyond the rays to a figure sitting in shadow across the way.

"What happened, Pete?"

"You got sideswiped," he said, remaining motionless in his chair. "Consider yourself fortunate. The doctor says it was a mild concussion. They gave you a sedative and held you overnight for observation."

The good news did not match the subdued tone of Pete's voice. Glaringly missing was the banter normally directed his way.

"How's Eva?" Adam asked. "I tried to pull her from the

vehicle's path but that's when the lights went out."

"You need to improve your technique of grabbing hold of women in peril" he expected his boss to say, wanted him to say it.

Instead, Pete rose from his chair and slowly passed through the sunbeams like a messenger from the celestial world, emerging at the edge of his bed. "She's dead, Adam," he replied.

He closed his eyes in a feeble effort to return to the darkness he moments before awakened from, the darkness where all human thought is put to rest.

"Holy hell, Pete," he said upon reopening them. "Holy, freaking hell."

"It was quick," his boss continued. "The coroner listed the cause as massive head injuries. She was found dead at the scene."

"The body is in the morgue?"

"Yes. The family is making arrangements to have her buried in Indiana where she was from."

Another young woman returning home in a box to a place she probably should never have left in the first place, Adam thought. "Does the family want to speak with me?"

"No. They simply want their daughter back and the person who did it to be caught"

His boss reached out and gave him a pat on the shoulder. "They do not fault you. They took the accident investigators' word it was a hit and run. They will receive a final report pending the investigators' interview with you, which could come any minute."

Pete returned to his chair. "You want to tell me what you recall before you recall it to them?"

"I didn't see much, other than bright headlights bearing down on us at a good pace as Eva was swinging the door open to get into my truck. The beams were riding high, so it could have been a truck or van. Do the investigators know?"

"There were two witnesses who heard the collision and saw a vehicle speeding away. And, yeah, it appeared to them it was a dark van."

"Strange thing is, I didn't hear any squealing or skidding tires."

"Any back and forth shifting of the beams?" Pete asked.

"No, they stayed in a direct trajectory toward us."

"Like he was not making any effort to avoid you."

"Right."

"Well, there's always the possibility the driver was drunk or fell asleep at the wheel," his boss suggested.

"In either case he would have been weaving or in a drift, Adam replied. "No, this guy was making a beeline."

"Let's hope they find the vehicle, and speaking of vehicles, you're truck is in the police garage where it's being held for evidence. I took the liberty of getting you a rental replacement. It's at the office.

"What time is it?" he asked, as if it mattered.

"Ten o'clock or thereabouts," his boss answered, not bothering to check his watch.

Pete again rose from his chair and walked to the window for a glance outside before turning to face him. "So, how do you feel?"

"How am I supposed to feel? Other than a headache, I don't know. Guilty? Lucky? Sad? Puzzled? Pissed?" Take your pick.

Why couldn't he have been the cad he was with her all along and turned down her request for a ride?

"I like the pissed part," Pete said. "It means you'll be back to work tomorrow. By the way, your professor called a short while ago from the college to check on you. Apparently, she got word of the accident through the school. She was going to make a trip down but I assured her you were fine and about to be released."

"Did she see anything?"

"Last night?"

"Yes."

"Nothing. Said it all happened after she left."

"Can you adjust this thing to the sit-up position?" Adam asked, nodding to the underside of the bed.

Pete reached to wind the handle several rotations. "She said she would understand if you decided to skip class," he said.

"I'll be there."

"One another thing, I contacted your parents to advise them of your situation. They are expecting a call from you."

The echo of footsteps in the hallway drew their attention to the doorway. Two uniformed officers, each carrying a clipboard, paused to check the room number before entering. For a half hour Adam repeated to them what he essentially told Pete. An hour later he was released from the hospital.

CHAPTER NINE

"Senior citizen discounts! Where did you come up with that idea?" Pete asked, turning to Adam with a feigned quizzical look on his face.

His boss appeared ready to resume the banter between the two following a daylong moratorium. Adam wasn't quite up to it, however, as Eva's death cry still reverberated within him. "I didn't. An elderly gent called in a while ago to ask if we offered them."

"No thank you. All we need is the Florida geezer nation lining up at our door with their coupons in hand like there was an early-bird special going on," he said. "I tell you we would be up to our necks doing background checks on the grandkids' nannies, the fellows at the senior singles clubs, the suspicious house maids, or whomever. Never trust anyone under seventy is how they think, except if you are a phone scammer, then they're all too trusting in you."

Peterson worked the computer in feverish fashion, slipping in floppies he received from a real estate buddy in the Keys listing commercial properties up for sale. His drive toward his dream was picking up pace, perhaps due to the pressure of recent events. Any grand notions he may have had of growing his business apparently were out the window, as he sought to glide the firm in for a soft landing while he still had the time.

"Okay, how about the other end of the age scale?" Adam asked from across the desk. "I had a promoter call in today who was looking for a bodyguard this weekend for a rocker who is coming to town for a concert date. Seems his regular guy took sick and he needs a substitute."

"Again, no thanks," he said, keeping his eyes fastened to the computer screen.

"Said he would pay a hundred bucks an hour."

"Still no thanks. If you plan on doing bodyguard work, you'd better plan on packing a firearm. I retired mine years ago when I gave up the risky side of the business."

The subject of weapons never came up between the two, though admittedly the matter crossed Adam's mind when he first came on board. It quickly became evident, however, that the image of the private eye fashioned by Hollywood fell several figments short of reality.

"I meant to ask you when I was going to be issued my Barney Fife bullet," Adam said, managing some mirth.

"The day Barney drops by to hand it to you," Peterson said, printing out a final page from the computer and leaning back in his chair. "Speaking of risky business, I saw an out-of-towner driving around in a van the other day with the moniker Infidelity Investigations, Inc. bannered on its side. Just goes to show you how specialization is taking hold. Can you picture that thing pulling up in front of somebody's house like a repair truck? Sure to get the neighbors talking, don't you think?"

"Not exactly an undercover operation he is conducting," Adam responded. "He either has a back-up van for his field work or else he's turned the risk-reward ration on its head."

Peterson clasped his hands behind his neck. "You know, I once knew a risk manager. The guy had an obsession with odds.

Everything in life involved a risk, he would say, whether it was on the job or off. So he started compiling this list of activities—driving, flying, skiing, bicycle riding, mowing the lawn—everything you could imagine. He then would set the odds on the chances of a serious or fatal accident occurring during the performance of each activity."

"Based on what?"

"Based on accurate historical data," he claimed. "He also broke it down by profession—cop, fireman, soldier, miner, whatever. Apparently, that's what risk managers do—sit around and think of odds and occupations."

"What were the odds for private eyes?"

"I didn't ask. I figured it was something I didn't need to know," Peterson said, leaning his face down to blow some dust particles off the desk. "Does the cleaning crew ever dust around here?"

"Did he put a time frame on those odds of his?" Adam asked.

"Sure did. Like the odds of having a car accident within five years were such and such, the odds of getting killed in military combat were this and that, and so on. The guy kept adding activities to his lists till he had enough to fill a book, which is what he ended up doing—compiling a loose-leaf book. He carried the thing around with him wherever he went, continually checking it like a football coach does with his playbook on the sidelines. He claimed it would become the bible of the risk management industry."

"Did he find a publisher?"

"Nope. From what I hear he was killed in an accident before he could shop it around. An industrial tractor backed over him while he had his head in the book."

"Too bad he didn't have anything in there about the dangers of reading," he said.

"Yeah, but he died doing what he loved best," his boss quipped.

A choice denied his classmate Adam could not help but think.

*

Adam dialed the number for the Estuary Preservation Society and asked for the date and time of their next meeting.

"As a matter of fact, we are holding a public reception this evening for individuals interested in joining or learning about our organization," the lady on the other end of the line advised him.

"Where and what time?" he asked.

"Seven tonight at the Harborside Hall on the downtown waterfront," she replied.

"Thank you," he said, pleased with the timing. For once he wouldn't have to top off his gas tank to chase down a lead.

He arrived at the hall, a conical-shaped structure resembling a stand-alone small college gym, at half past seven. A statuesque woman with lacquered-on black hair and pale complexion and dressed in a floor-length lavender dress greeted him at the entrance. Handing him a program sheet, she directed him into the main hall with a smile and gentle gesture of the hand. Inside, lines of skinny plastic folding tables, covered with an array of promotional materials, were arranged in the middle of the floor. Overhead, a giant green and yellow banner hung from the ceiling, welcoming visitors. Several other tables, covered with bright green tablecloths, were positioned against a wall and lined with drinks and snacks, including coffee, tea, sodas, bottled water, cookies, brownies, and various cheeses. Clusters of guests were milling about the tables, picking and poking at the foods and pamphlets.

He was about to take a bite out of one of the brownies when the woman who escorted him into the room drew to his side.

"Are you a member of the organization?" she asked, delivering it as if she already knew the answer.

He lowered the brownie. "No, I'm not a member."

He prepared himself for the pitch to join but realized it was the price he would have to pay for admission.

"As you will see from our pamphlets and brochures, we are involved in a variety of estuary preservation activities," she said, gesturing to the non-food tables.

"You're involved in both restoration and preservation?" Adam asked, trailing her down a row of tables past other browsers.

"Yes, our primary goal is to eventually restore a balance to the Tampa Bay estuary by implementing programs to remove invasive species and clear aquatic debris—activities along those lines," she said, looking over her shoulder. "We also conduct research programs and maintain a student endowment fund."

"How long has this organization been in existence?" he asked, feeling comfortable enough to take a bite out of the brownie.

"Oh, ten years or so," she said, ending their stroll. "I wasn't here from the beginning. I joined five years ago."

"Did you know of a woman by the name of Carlene Wheeler?" he asked, casually finishing off the snack.

She thought for a moment. "I didn't know her on a personal level but knew of her. She was one of the founding members of the society. Perhaps you heard she was killed years ago in the Skyway Bridge collapse. It was a great loss to the organization from what I hear. Were you a friend of hers?"

"More like an acquaintance. I read that she was honored for her activities with this group and I was interested in learning more about her contributions."

"Then you should talk to Shelia Watson, the vice-president of our organization. She was a good friend of hers, from what I understand."

He glanced around the floor. "She here tonight?"

"Yes. See the woman across the way in the pumpkin-colored pantsuit, the one with the short auburn hair?" she asked, pointing a finger.

"The one talking to the man in the blue shirt?"

"Yes, the lady with the drink in her hand. That's her," she said.

From his vantage point, she appeared to be the same woman who was presenting Carlene Wheeler her award in the photo he dug up in the library. Excusing himself, he ambled slowly toward the couple, taking his time perusing the tables until he noticed the blue-shirt guy and vice-president part ways. Seeing his opening he approached her, saying the lady in the long skirt across the room referred him to her.

"I'm told you were a friend of Carlene Wheeler," he said.

She wore a sheepish smile on her finely featured face, the permanent kind that often conceals a steely interior.

"Yes, I was," she said in a confident voice. "You knew Carlene?"

"I knew her by way of her old home town of Hidden Valley, Ohio. I also am a transplant from up north and recall reading about her association with your organization. I have taken an interest in various environmental issues through the years and thought I'd check into your program."

"Your name?" she asked.

"Adam Fraley," he answered, forsaking a pseudonym in case she asked for an occupation, which he was prepared to tell her. As far as he knew, private investigators were not reputed to be hostile to environmental causes and it was not out of the question one could show up for such an event. Furthermore, he was confident his being there would not cause additional trouble for Pete. "Terrible thing to happen to Carlene, wasn't it?"

She looked at him deadpanned through her chiseled smile. "I could exercise a little black humor and say she ended up dying in the arms of the thing she loved the most."

"The bay?"

"The bay, despite her aversion to crossing it by way of the bridge."

Adam liked this woman.

"You would call her a driving force behind the group?" he asked.

She took a sip of her drink before continuing. "Carlene did as much as anyone to get this organization off the ground. She was one of those people who didn't mind getting her hands dirty doing good works. She also wasn't one of those transplants who leave their loyalties up north. You know the kind, Mr. Fraley, the ones who hole up in condos and gaited enclaves and never take an interest in the local community, the ones who can't find their way downtown after living here five years. Carlene wasn't like that. She wanted to contribute from the beginning and did so with style and substance. For someone who had to bear as many burdens as she did, it was quite an accomplishment."

"I hear she faced a tough battle with cancer as well."

"Yes, only to have the ship and bridge finish what it couldn't."

"How did her husband hold up under it all?" he asked.

She halted the movement of her drink to her mouth. "He held up fine. He just wasn't any good at holding her up."

He gave her a perplexed look.

"Before I respond, maybe I should ask if you are a friend of his."

"No."

She took another drink and carefully set her glass on a nearby table. "Mr. Wheeler and I did not get along," she said. "He was the controlling type, meaning he not only attempted to control his wife but also those around her, including me. He looked upon me as a kind of co-conspirator of hers, somebody responsible for getting her involved in an organization that served as an oasis in her life, a place where she could express her talents freely."

He imagined this formidable-looking woman and Wheeler locking horns. "He was opposed to her being a member?"

"He went along with it because he wanted her to play the role of the politician's wife, someone who would involve herself in civic causes to help boost his public image. It was not her intent in undertaking the project but it was his in letting her do so."

"Her illness must have had a crushing impact on both her and the organization."

"The organization held up well, primarily because of the solid foundation she helped build. She herself did not hold up as well, primarily because of him. I was her closest friend. As such she would confide in me the constant mental abuse she endured."

"During her illness?"

She hesitated before answering, as though she might be betraying a loyalty to her former friend. "Especially during her illness. In fact, on one of her darkest days, she broke down in tears, telling me her husband was trying to have her committed to a nursing home."

"She felt it wasn't necessary, I take it."

"She didn't and I didn't. He simply saw her as a burden to delegate to someone else. Of course he was trying to work it all out behind the scenes without anyone's knowledge so not to cause embarrassment for the family—his side of the family in particular."

"Wasn't her sister living here at the time?"

"Yes…Charlene was her name. I met her on a couple of occasions."

"Wasn't she able to lend a helping hand?"

"She really wasn't in a position to help. She was fairly new to the area and struggling to get on her feet. Actually, it was Carlene who was helping her up until her illness."

"She had no influence on Carlene's husband?"

"Charlene was the little sister, pretty to look at and a bit naïve in my view. She certainly wasn't the type to break Monte Wheeler's stranglehold on his wife."

"But Carlene's health improved."

"Yes it did. It almost had to if she was to avoid being institutionalized. It was like she willed herself to better health."

"Were you aware her sister committed suicide a short while back?"

Her face froze in surprise. "No, I was not. After Carlene's death I had no further contact with the family," she said, softening her tone.

"She jumped from the Skyway Bridge seven years to the day her sister died."

She shook her head. "Unbelievable how that family has been decimated. Was this in the paper? Monte Wheeler's paper?" she asked derisively. "If so, I missed it."

"There was an article," Adam said, leaving it at that.

He noticed two women waving to her from across the room, catching her attention.

"Well, I 'm going to have to excuse myself to do some mingling," she said, nodding to the gathering guests and taking her drink back in hand. "Part of my job for the night."

She wandered off, melting into the drift of visitors, at which point he took one last glance around at Carlene's creation and left, stopping by a food table to grab another brownie on his way out.

*

He arrived at class with decidedly mixed feelings. On the one hand, there was his instructor he looked forward to seeing; on the other there was an empty chair to face.

Prior to the start of class, the professor offered a few consoling words on the passing of their classmate, underscoring the shock of it all. She made no mention of Adam's role in the incident, though he was sure others in the room were made aware of it through news accounts or word of mouth. At one student's suggestion, it was agreed the class would send flowers. It was the least they could do.

Once into the session, the professor appeared no less her normal self, delivering the lesson plan with all the professional aplomb she demonstrated in the past. And what was he expecting? An extra glance his way, followed by a locking of eyes, followed by an elbow in the ribs from Eva? He glanced at the empty chair still sitting next to him.

At the close of class, he finally received the look he was waiting for, the one indicating she wanted to see him.

"I made a dumb mistake," she said, as soon as the room cleared. "It goes to show just how absentminded professors can be. I set aside my reporter's notes on the bridge incident this morning fully intending to bring them to class but instead walked off without them."

Her focus left no doubt she had put the coffee shop tragedy behind her. He had forgotten about the reporter's notes. In his one-track mind those notes had been usurped by the notes exchanged between the two of them at the coffee house.

"Listen, I know we traded subjects, but I still would like for you to review them to see if there are any inconsistencies with your version of events," she said in earnest. "I don't live far from here. If you don't mind following me home, I could show them to you."

"Sure," he said, enticed as much by the invitation as by the notes.

He trailed her red Mustang to a section of town popular with young professionals on the lookout for central city restoration projects. No sooner had they turned onto Longfellow Lane, an oak-tree-canopied street bisecting the quiet neighborhood, than a boom box reverberating from a dark van riding his tail broke the stillness of the night. In an instant his mind was back at the coffee shop. A half-block later, his teacher wheeled her Mustang into a driveway, leaving him room to pull in behind her. As if acting in unison, the van in turn swung into a driveway further down the block before disappearing between houses, its beat still audible.

"Can you imagine how that must sound inside the van?" she commented on exiting her car.

They strode across a strip of concrete walkway leading from the driveway to the front of a tall, narrow clapboard house with tall, narrow windows. "Nice place," he said, following her onto a wooden porch featuring a rocking chair and swing.

"I can't believe I forgot the folder," she said, turning the lock on the front door.

She led him into a tiny entry foyer fronting a wooden staircase. Off to the side was an opened parlor that had been converted into an office space.

"The folder is lying on the desk," she said, pointing into the parlor. "Now, if you'll excuse me, I'm going to run upstairs for a quick fresh-up while you get started."

Furnished with a matching mahogany desk, side table, and glass bookcase full of glossy, leather-bound books, the office was in immaculate shape, not a condition one normally would associate with absentminded professors—or journalists, for that matter.

He took the folder from the desk, sat down at the table, and emptied its contents before him. The notes were random, scribbled on sheets of yellow legal pad from top to bottom. Many were lifted from the medical examiner's report, citing no evidence of a pre-existing medical condition or drugs in Charlene's system. Also included were details of the injuries suffered from the impact: massive bleeding from both ears, broken ribs, torn spleen, cracked vertebrae, ruptured liver. It was not the image of her he cared to conjure up. Other notations made mention of the lack of a suicide note, missing handbag, the victim being an Ohio native, and the presence of a single witness who could offer no more than what was in the official finding. As expected, there was no mention of a sister having died in the exact same location. Attached to the folder was a copy of the sheriff's report.

He was on the second scan-through of the notes, making sure he had not overlooked an item, when he heard her footsteps on the staircase.

"Sorry for the delay," she said, entering the room. "How are you coming along?"

She had changed into a beige t-shirt, faded jeans, and sandals, a casual side of her he heretofore could only imagine.

He pointed to the bottom of one of the sheets. "It's mainly a rehash of what we already know, though there are a few references I don't quite understand."

She slid into a chair alongside him for a closer view, a fresh-out-of-the-shower scent accompanying her. "What references are those?"

He pointed to the sheet. "If I read these right, they say pizza place, yogurt shop, souvenir shop, computer store, copy center, flower shop, deli, laundry, and travel agency. He has check-marked them all. What are they in reference to, any idea?"

"Yes, I asked him about them. They are stores located in a small shopping plaza located between the southern end of the bridge and Bradenton. I believe it is called the Southwest Shopping Plaza. People who are traveling south of the bridge often use it as a pit stop. Our guy thought it a good idea to check the stores on the chance Miss Gibbs may have stopped in one of them for whatever reason. Nobody seemed to recall her, though."

"But he was working on the assumption she was traveling alone, correct?"

"Correct," she said, raising her eyes from the paper to him.

"So, he was inquiring about her, not Wheeler," he said, underscoring the point.

"It would be interesting to know why they were traveling south," she said. "It is really no place to be day-tripping, unless they were just out for a drive or going for a walk. Bay View Park is close by. Maybe they were planning an outing there."

"He booked the rental car for two days. He could have been planning an overnight stay," he suggested.

"Why then were they headed back at such a late hour?" she asked.

"A blow-up could have occurred. The fact there were no drugs found in her system indicates she was off her meds."

"I'll have my reporter check the hotel registrations along the highway to Bradenton," she said.

"He can do that?"

"We do have our ways, Mr. Fraley," she said. "Don't worry, it's all legal."

He wondered if it was anything like his boss's way. Get on the phone, make like you're Wheeler, tell them you spent a certain night there, and could they call your name up on their computer to

160

verify if you had the right night recorded in your official travel record.

"Worth a check, though I don't think it's a likely scenario," he said. "If they wanted to spend the night together, they could have gone to her place."

"Why did the blow-up occur that evening, I suppose is the question, or was it simply a culmination of events?" she asked.

"I have a question for you," Adam said, shifting his chair to face her directly, his knee slightly brushing her thigh. "What do people first do when they receive an important document in hand? And don't say read it."

She rested her elbow on the table and cupped her hand under her chin. "Store it away in a safe place, like a safe, I suppose."

"Even before they put it there, what are they likely to do?"

"Make a copy of it?"

The look on his face gave her the answer.

She released her chin from her hand. "Are you referring to the affidavit?" she asked, widening her eyes.

"Obviously, stuff had been simmering between the two for some time. What is most likely to have precipitated a blow-up, given what we know about Charlene's intention, since arriving back in Tampa?"

"The heart of the matter, or the offspring of the affair, to be precise," she said. "It had to be unsettling. And that raises another question. Why would Charlene be so intent on her daughter knowing who her biological father was, when it was her sister's husband after all? Don't you think it would be something she would want to keep from her, if at all possible?"

"That's the tragedy of it all. Her thought process was skewed...stuck on a single goal...to give validation to her life and child in the most fundamental way she knew how. It must have come as some consolation to her for the pregnancy to occur after her sister's death or else the thought of her grown daughter doing the math would have really posed a quandary for her. Remember also, it was the anniversary day of her sister's death, something I'm sure was playing on her mind during her outing with Wheeler."

"So, you now feel the end game is near," she said.

"Yes, I plan on retracing your reporter's steps, knowing what we now know," he said.

"You are not forgetting our trade agreement, are you?"

This time he gave no reaction for her to gauge.

"Ever have need for a private investigator, Miss Egan?" he asked.

"For me personally or for the paper?"

"Either."

She raised her eyes in thought. "Actually, there was an incident in my past resembling in many aspects the Charlene Gibbs case."

"Oh yeah? Tell me."

"It dates back to my first newspaper job," she said. "I was working for a daily in the small town of Ravenwood, Illinois. It's about a hundred miles south of Chicago. The paper is called the *Ravenwood Observer*. It was the one run by the son of the publisher I was telling you about. At the time I was fresh out of journalism school and working my first job as a sports writer. While there, I befriended the wire editor, another new employee who had come on board the same week I had. Anyway, about three months into the job, a personal tragedy struck the organization. Getting ready to open shop one Monday morning, we learned the wife of the paper's business manager had died quite unexpectedly over the weekend. The tragedy was they were a very young couple, each in their twenties."

"Died from what?" he asked.

"That was the question we were all asking. Word had spread among the staff in days leading up to her death that she was ill but never were we led to believe it was a life-threatening condition. The flu had hit the town and everyone assumed she was down with a severe case of it."

"How well did you know them?"

"The business office was separated from the newsroom. However, the *Observer* was a small paper where everyone eventually came to know each other, even if only on a surface level. His wife I didn't know, though I had seen her on several occasions around town with her husband."

"So, are you saying it was a mysterious death or a suspicious one?" he asked.

"The rumor mill definitely pegged it as a mysterious one. Apparently, authorities could not determine the exact cause of death, other than to say it was related in some manner to a virus. Needless to say, it put the staff on edge for a while."

"And when did the suspicion set in?"

"The suspicion arrived by way of my wire-editor friend. He was from Chicago and would try and make it up there on weekends whenever the opportunity arose. Less than a month after the death of his wife, the business manager offered my friend a lift to the city, saying he was headed up there for a weekend getaway. My friend said fine, it would save him some wear and tear on his car and provide him some company. Well, my friend later told me the kind of news you really don't want to hear."

"The kind I *want* to hear," Adam said, interrupting her with a grin.

She laid a hand on her knee and smiled faintly. "Yes, the kind you are now going to hear," she said, as if anxious to get it off her chest. "He said on the drive up they at one point stopped for gas when the business manager pulled out his billfold and plucked from it a photo of a young woman he described as his girlfriend. According to my friend, the woman was dressed in a cocktail waitress uniform, a very revealing one. It turns out he met her at a private club he had been patronizing. My friend said the guy was very anxious for him to see the photo, as if he wanted to display his newly-won trophy to him."

"A very male thing," he interjected.

"And all coming less than a month after his wife's death," she said.

"Leading to suspicious minds. Anything come of it?"

"No. A small newspaper operation is similar to any other small business. By nature there are few degrees of separation among staff, except if the publisher is off traveling the world. Normally, it is like family. You are reluctant to turn on one another, especially if you are new and have only a whiff of suspicion and not any solid evidence. To get back to your original question, my friend threw out the idea to me of hiring a private investigator to check into the situation but we never followed through on it. Not long after, I accepted a position with my father's old newspaper. A year later I happened to be traveling through Ravenwood and dropped by the *Observer* for a visit. My friend was still there. He informed me the business manager left his job a few months earlier to take a position in Chicago."

"To live happily ever after?"

"I suppose. I soon left the matter behind me, convinced it was an issue beyond my control. You bringing the Gibbs case to my attention resurrected the matter in my mind and raised some questions regarding how a potentially sticky story should be handled."

"Or whether it should be handled at all," he said.

She looked at him thoughtfully. "Right. Looking at the incident in hindsight posed the question whether we in the news business abide by our own standards when faced with difficult internal matters," she said, turning her gaze from him to empty space.

Her reflective mood was captured in her face, casting it in a mature light, one to compliment her natural beauty. Any mask she may have been wearing or any air she may have adopted was now shed following her trip into the past.

She steepled her fingers together, tracing them along her lips before abruptly lowering them. "You know, after our discussion the other evening, the idea of hiring you on as a stringer popped into my mind on the way home," she said. "It would be one way for us to give you a legitimate byline on the story."

"A stringer is a freelance reporter, right?"

"Right."

"By the way, who came up with the term?" he asked. "It wasn't something I missed in class, was it?"

"Not in this class. It dates back to the days when part-time reporters were paid by the amount of their copy the newspaper ended up printing. At the close of the pay period, someone on the paper would measure the length of the freelancer's copy by a string. The writer then would be paid according to the length of the string, thus the origin of the term. Editors do not want to get stuck with a lot of blank space to fill on a page after all of the advertising slots have been accounted for. Therefore, the stringers' stories come in handy."

"What sorts of stories?" he asked.

"Social and civic club activities, college and high school events, church gatherings, the list is endless. It's also a good way for someone to get a foothold in the business."

"I may have much to learn about journalism, but I consider the bridge incident story to be several rungs in importance above the stringer type you describe; therefore I'm holding you to the trade. Having said that, I would still like to retrace your reporter's path, if you have no objection."

"No objection at all. I understand your interest in the story. I only ask you keep me informed of your findings or observations," she said, the hint of a smile forming on the corners of her lips.

Her bringing to mind the exchange of notes at Breakers brought a pause to the discussion, one of those awkward moments when locked eyes look for a direction to take the conversation. And hers were not just any pair of eyes. Radiating intelligence, they seemed capable of processing information at the least indication of it.

"Well, it's getting late," she said, pressing her palms down on the front edge of her chair, as if ready to abandon it.

He welcomed the move for it likely saved him from saying or doing something very foolish.

She walked him to the front porch, reminding him of his ladies-in-the-locker-room assignment and her willingness to contribute background information should he desire such, an offer he immediately bumped to the top of his priority list. What to make of it, he asked himself, while backing out of the drive. No sooner had the question arisen than another replaced it. What was the van that followed him down the block and ducked between houses earlier in the evening now doing out on Longfellow Lane parked among other cars?

He steered his pickup past the vehicle, attempting to appear normal in his movements while at the same time keeping on the lookout for signs of life inside the van. Not surprisingly, its windows were tinted except for the rear ones, which were closed to outside view by mini curtains. He looked for dents or scratches but detected none. Once beyond the van he circled to the next block over, parking his truck halfway down the street. For the next few minutes, he kicked himself for not noting the license plate. He then circled back to discover the van was gone but not his suspicion.

*

"I thought you dropped the bridge incident matter," Peterson said, vigorously shaking the last drops of a water bottle into one of the office planters.

"As a commercial matter, yes, but there is a civil side to it," he said from his desk chair, his hands clasped behind his head.

"Civil as in civil court or civil as in civil behavior?"

"The latter," he replied.

Peterson walked from across the room to exchange his empty bottle for one of the full ones he had lined up on top of the desk.

"Is she going to run the story in the *Gazette*?"

"Maybe…maybe not."

He watched his boss flit from planter to planter, tending to his plants. "Don't they take the minerals out of that purified stuff?" he asked. "What good is it for the plants?"

"Does it look like they're hurting?" Peterson replied, continuing his watering. Halfway between planters he paused and took a sweeping view of the office. "You know, I've been thinking. What say we get a cockatoo or two for this place?" he asked. "We could stick them in the corners."

"If you're asking for my vote—it's no. First of all, bird maintenance is not in my job description. Secondly, I'll be the one having to sit here and listen to their screams."

"Maybe macaws would be better, though I hear those things are damn expensive," he said.

Adam picked up the empty bottles and tossed them into a recycling bin. "What do you make of the van?" he asked, getting his boss back on track.

"A surveillance job, I expect."

"Why would he come blaring up behind me and why park out front?"

"There are those who hold to the theory it is better to be brazen in your approach, since it's not what is expected of a snoop. All depends on the conditions. As for the second part of your question, it was a naked setting, right? No shrubs or trees to peek through or around. Under those circumstances the snoop has no choice but to raise his risk level. He had no idea how long you were going to be in there, but he sure as hell wasn't going to miss you walking out with her and at the same time the chance at a compromising photo. By the way, he didn't get one, did he?"

"No," he said adamantly.

"Don't be sure. The way I see it a student accompanies his teacher to her house late in the evening, spends some time there doing who knows what..."

"Talking business in the parlor room," Adam interjected.

"...talking in the parlor room. Does the parlor room have windows?"

"Yes."

"Were the curtains or blinds drawn?"

"No."

"Were you sitting across from her or next to her?"

"We were looking over some notes together...yes, next to each other."

Peterson finished his watering and returned to the desk. "So you were nose to nose for camera angle purposes, maybe even smooching. Anything else?"

"There is one other circumstance I should mention," he said.

"Okay, mention it."

"When we first arrived, she took a few minutes to run upstairs for a quick shower and change of clothes."

"Great. Let's hope she at least had her bathroom curtains drawn. Even so, you've got your teacher entering the house with you when she's wearing one set of clothes and exiting wearing another."

"We're adults, Pete. This isn't a high school situation we are talking about. Besides, is there not a privacy issue involved in aiming a camera inside a home without the owner's permission?"

"Yes, indeed. Still, the situation you describe is likely to not sit well with biased observers or classmates, much less school officials, even if it's only photos of you entering and leaving that turn up."

"If it was a tail, it had to be Wheeler who was behind it," he said.

"How does Wheeler tie in with the teacher?"

"When I went to interview him, I let him know I was a student at Live Oak. He easily could have checked on who my instructor was. He also had an added interest once he discovered who it was, since she had applied several years ago for a position he had vacated at the *Beacon*. Turned out he was a member of the panel who interviewed her for the job. Also, if he had a tail on us, he undoubtedly would have heard about our get-together at Breakers when I discussed the bridge incident with her."

"It begs the question," Pete said. "Is there a Wheeler connection to the van that sideswiped you the same night?"

"Not sure it's his style. Besides, the sequence doesn't make sense. Why send a hired hand to nearly kill you and then settle for revealing photos when the first attempt fails."

"Could be the hired hand bungled the task. Maybe he was sent to give you a warning tap and missed the mark."

Adam shook his head. "I'd hate to think Eva got caught in the middle of this. It's bad enough I drug my professor into it."

"You got a thing going with 'Teach,' Adam?"

"No, I haven't 'got a thing going with Teach.'"

"Do you wish you had a thing going with her?"

He narrowed his eyes and flashed his boss a don't-go-there look.

"She's now in Wheeler's cross-hairs, Adam, one way or the other. Tell me, what kind of a woman is she?"

"What kind of a woman?"

"Yes, and don't recite to me the usual male litany of body parts and functions. Tell me instead how she carries herself."

He thought for a moment, picturing her in front of the class in one of her pastel suits with one hand resting easy on one hip and the other half way into the air to emphasize a point. "I would say she carries herself with an air of independence."

Peterson leaned back in his chair and threw his hands high, clapping them once in appreciation. "There you go, Adam, the kind of woman who, without uttering a word, sends a guy the message you've got to have a lot of luck to get lucky with me."

"What does that have to do with anything?"

"It means she is someone you can go into battle with. Someone who has confidence."

"Well, the situation does seem to be ratcheting up. I'll grant you that," he said.

"When you reach the stage where you have private eyes tailing private eyes, you know it's so. All you have to do is look at the

Church of Scientology situation over in Clearwater where you have snoops for loyal church members and disgruntled ex-members crossing paths on a daily basis."

"Until we know the photos actually exist, there's not a lot we can do about them," he said in a dejected tone.

"Oh, but there is," his boss countered. "It's called a preemptive move. You can get on the phone and tell your teacher to immediately get in touch with her supervisors at the school to explain to them the situation. It does a world of good for them to hear it first from her. It gives them the opportunity to legitimize it by saying they already were aware of the circumstances leading to your dropping by her house. In other words, there was nothing confidential about it at all."

He wasted no time in following Peterson's advice, reaching her by phone at her newspaper office. Whether she was surprised, skeptical, embarrassed, or peeved by the conjecture, she was not letting on, maintaining a neutral tone throughout the call. "For propriety's sake it wouldn't be a bad idea to meet in the *Gazette* office from now on," she said, while acknowledging the wisdom of Peterson's suggestion to touch base with her superiors. In a footnote to the conversation she also advised him they had checked the hotel registrations as she promised and came up empty.

Later, Adam ducked out of the office to make a quick trip to the library to try and dig up a more current photo of Monte Wheeler to take with him to the shopping plaza the next morning. He found one in a local magazine story featuring the *Beacon* editor receiving a citizen-of-the-year award from a civic group. He obtained a photocopy of it, not the best of reproductions, but passable. On the way back to the office he stopped at a downtown drive-in restaurant where a girl in an orange-and-white pinstriped uniform with curly blonde locks flowing from beneath her cap delivered him a hamburger loaded with tomato sauce, lettuce, pickles, and onions. He devoured it while staring at the photo of a smiling Wheeler he had placed on the passenger seat..

Arriving back at the office, he unexpectedly found Peterson there to greet him. Judging by the sour look on his face, his boss was about to bear him some bad news.

"Got a call from a guy by the name of Gary Merkel. Ever hear of him?" he asked.

"The name sounds vaguely familiar," Adam said.

"He's the lead investigative reporter for the *Beacon*."

"Oh, yeah," he said, the name becoming more familiar when linked to the paper.

"Whenever you see his byline, you know it's going to be front page material with damning stuff to follow. The guy has won all sorts of awards for his work"

"What did he want?" he asked.

"Says he's working on a story having to do with private investigation agencies, specifically the delicate lines they walk between legal and illegal activities."

"What sorts of illegal activities?"

"Accessing confidential records, withholding evidence, posing as law enforcement officials, attempting to deceive or defraud the public, interfering with lawful investigations, and so on, all of which are grounds for having a license revoked or suspended," his boss said somberly.

"And none of which we have done."

"Close counts in this game, Adam. It only takes a shading of the facts to have us appear to have crossed the line. You were a student on assignment when you interviewed Wheeler, but you were also an employee of mine. You were an insurance claims representative when you were checking on the bridge tapes, but you also were on the Peterson payroll. You were a representative of the Gibbs family when you were checking into her background, yet at the same time an employee of this agency even if you were officially off duty."

And you were Monte Wheeler checking into rental car records Adam wanted to add, but didn't.

"Those are half-truths, Pete, as you well know."

"Which halves of the truth do you think will make it into print?"

"So Wheeler is doing his own preemptive strike."

"He sees us as a fly on his fiefdom, so he's about to bring out the giant swatter."

"When do they plan on running this series?"

"He didn't say. I suspect it depends on how Wheeler takes stock of events."

"How do you think he sees them at the moment?"

"He obviously knows what you and your teacher are cooking up and the hand you have to play. I don't mind calling it a weak one, if your intent is to draw him into the story. Right now, all you have is the tale of a woman jumping to her death at a spot where seven years earlier her sister was killed in one of this area's worst disasters. He thinks it is of no business to the public, not because of personal family reasons, but because it would shine the spotlight on him and raise embarrassing questions, not the least of which is the killer one of why he buried the story. As we talked about before, the protecting-the-family-privacy line doesn't apply to public figures in a matter like this. You can bet it wouldn't sit well with his colleagues or superiors, not to mention his wife and father-in-law."

Peterson screwed the cap off another water bottle, tossed it into a bin, and took a long drink, obviously attempting to quench his nerves. "You know what one of people's worst fears is?" he asked.

"I hear giving a speech is right up there," he said, not giving it much thought.

"That and waking up in the morning to see your name splattered on the front page of the paper. Nine times out of ten, it won't be for good reasons. To say it is a kick in the stomach is an understatement, considering you have worked for nearly thirty years to build and preserve a reputable one."

No question Adam had far less on the line in this fight than his boss or teacher, a fact made plain by the palpable pall hanging over the room. Never, in his brief time on the job, had he seen his mentor display his serious side to this degree.

"We're a small business, Adam—very small," he said, leaning back and sliding his fingers through his hair. "We don't have a lot of weapons to wield, like a houseful of attorneys, when it comes to corporate power plays."

"We do have one weapon, Pete," he responded.

"What's that?"

"The truth."

Peterson crossed his arms across his chest, looked him directly in the eye, and managed a smile. "It's one of the reasons I hired you, Adam. You have an itch for the truth. Fortunately or unfortunately, in our business you have to demonstrate it."

He nodded his agreement.

"You got any gas in that rental of yours?" his boss asked, jerking his mind away from the *Beacon* reporter. "My wife has the car today and we need to take a trip over to Clearwater."

"Business trip?"

"Yeah, a business trip. You can put it on your expense account. We need to visit an instructor of yours."

*

They were traveling west on Gulf-to-Bay Boulevard, past an endless stretch of non-descript storefronts bordering both sides of the avenue when Peterson directed him to pull into a black asphalt parking lot siding a block of stores set back a short distance from the road.

"Is that the one?" Peterson asked, pointing to a van parked at the end of the lot in the guest slot.

"That's it," he said, swinging his truck in beside it.

They walked down a narrow concrete path to a lime-green clapboard storefront with the words Ronald Weeks Agency arching across its front window in chartreuse lettering. He followed his boss through the front door into a modest one-room office housing a reception desk, a waiting couch, a work desk, a small wooden conference table, and a hodgepodge of decorative items. On the walls were mounted a series of framed licenses and award certificates issued by professional organizations. Ronnie Weeks sat at the work desk in the back of the room, casually eyeing them as they made their entrance.

"Well if it isn't Pete Peterson," he said, rising to greet them. "And you are...?"

"Adam Fraley," he answered to a question his questioner already knew the answer to.

Weeks motioned them to the conference table where they each grabbed a chair.

"I'd ask what brings you out this way, Pete, but the minute you walked through the door I knew what this was about," he said, giving Peterson a friendly slap on the shoulder as he passed him by on the way to his seat. "I should have known not to send out a couple of rookies."

Peterson explained to him on the way over that the van incident had the signature of Ronnie Weeks all over it, the boldness of it, in particular. The guy was the renegade of the private eye business, flaunting conventional wisdom to keep a step ahead of the competition. "That isn't what he was selling at the surveillance seminar," he remarked to Peterson on hearing it. "Ronnie's known to veer from the playbook," his boss replied. "He just isn't going to broadcast it from the podium."

"You know Adam here works for me, don't you Ronnie?"

"I do now," he said, lacing his fingers together on the table.

"Your client didn't provide background info on your target?"

Weeks worked up a wry smile. "His target was the woman. I learned about Adam only this morning," he said, acknowledging him with a nod. "It was the reason I expected to hear from you."

On the ride over Peterson related how one private investigator eventually comes to recognize the style of a competitor in the same way a defensive back in football learns the moves of a wide receiver over the years. The first rule of warfare or any competition is to know your opponent, something Ronnie Weeks in a rare slip of judgment apparently failed to do. It usually occurs when you become too trusting of a client or so overwhelmed by their position in life you fail to question their motives, his boss explained.

"Why was the woman targeted?" Adam asked, feeling comfortable enough to enter the interplay between the two.

Weeks looked at him with a cock of his head and a flat expression. "Aren't we entering an area of confidence?" he asked, more as a statement than a query.

"Have you had the privilege of a visit from Gary Merkel recently, the investigative reporter for the *Beacon*?" his boss asked, redirecting the conversation.

Weeks leaned back in his chair and stuffed his hands in his pockets. "No. What's he up to?"

"He's doing a piece on private eye agencies. An investigative story to be precise."

"Investigating what?"

"Borderline legal practices."

"On your part?"

"So it seems."

"And you're thinking the snooping is somehow linked to Mr. Fraley and Miss Egan," Weeks said, glancing his way.

"For a fact, Ronnie," Peterson said. "Your client could have told you so, if he was of a mind to."

The guy was on the defensive and Peterson was not about to let him skate free. "Why was my employee targeted, Ronnie?"

"It's considered confidential information, Pete. You know that."

"Right now there is a crane with a demolition ball hanging from it parked outside my firm, Ronnie, ready to take a swing at it as soon as your client gives the word to Merkel," Peterson said.

From fly swatter to wrecking ball, his boss's imagery was

intensifying, he mused. For the moment he played spectator as the two veterans sat and stared at each other, having reached an impasse. Prying information out of Weeks on one of his clients was not going to be an easy task.

"How's Katie?" Peterson asked, breaking the lull and soon the impasse.

The question brought a slow smile to Weeks' face, as though he had been expecting it.

"Are you calling in your chip, Pete?" he asked.

The chip Adam also learned about on the drive over. It dated back a decade when Weeks had called on him for help in handling a personal matter involving his daughter Katie. At the time she had gone through a bitter divorce from a guy who had fought it all the way. Following his move out of the house, he began stalking her in a relentless manner, finally hurling the ultimate warning line at her, "If I can't have you no one will." To make matters worse, the guy was a cop who knew how to work the system to avoid detection and arrest. With the help of Peterson, Weeks compiled enough evidence to take his case to the local prosecutor who in turn presented it to his ex son-in-law's supervisor at the police department. The guy was given a choice, cease immediately with the stalking or else risk termination and possible prosecution. Faced with those options, even an obsessed stalker sometimes comes to his senses and in this case he did, fading out of the daughter's life.

"I'm down to my last one, Ronnie," Peterson said.

Weeks leaned forward in his chair and placed the palms of his hands on the table. "The woman was given to me as the target, Pete, not your assistant here. If I had known he worked for you, I wouldn't have taken the case. I was told he was a student, that's it."

"Why her?" Adam again asked, jumping in ahead of his boss.

"I was informed she was a major competitor of his who was trying to dig up dirt to throw at him for some reason. My client decided to dig faster. I'm still not sure what the core issue is, though I suspect you may be more tuned into it than I am."

"I'm sure you're aware of the hit-and-run at the Breakers involving Adam and another student," Peterson said. "Anything you can tell us about that."

"Only what I read in the paper. I have no other knowledge of it."

"Why focus on her academic workplace instead of the newspaper?" Peterson continued.

"My client said rumors were rampant she was playing around with students, if you know what I mean. He wanted me to check on it. That's when Mr. Fraley came into the picture," he said.

"Hardly a capital crime, even if true," Peterson remarked.

"As you know, Pete, you take what you can get in this business."

"And what did you get, Ronnie?" his boss asked.

Weeks hesitated a moment, pushed his lanky frame from the chair, ambled over to his desk, snatched a manila folder from a bottom drawer, and tossed it in front of them. "This is what we got," he said. "It's the only set in existence. The negatives are included. They're yours for the keeping."

Peterson opened the folder and emptied the black-and-white photos onto the table. There were no interior shots, just those of him and his teacher arriving and leaving, including a close-up one of him in his pickup as he drove by the van.

"How come we didn't have teachers like that in school, Pete?" he asked.

"Because we never made it to college, Ronnie."

Weeks rose from his chair. "I will inform my client I have uncovered all I can in this case," he said. "I'm sure there is much more at play here, more than I care to know about. So, as of now, consider us even, Pete. From here on you'll have to find another chip to play or else fold your hand."

"This isn't poker, Ronnie," his boss said, as they rose to leave.

"There's no folding in this game."

Peterson fell silent on the ride back, worry wrapping itself around him like a hungry boa around a captured lamb, choking the life out of it. He had won them a small victory, kept their heads free for the moment from the encircling threat. For how long was the question.

"Tell me again, Adam, what exactly did you see the night she jumped?" he asked, ending his silence.

"I told you what I saw, Pete."

"Then tell it to me again. I want to know everything from the beginning, and not just what was in the official report," he said, sounding like the boss who was taking over the job from the underling he no longer had confidence in.

"Everything?"

"Everything."

*

It was the one option he couldn't shake. Nine o'clock at night and rather than sitting in class pondering Hamlet's indecision, he was sitting in his truck outside his boss's villa battling his own uncertainty.

He had picked a quiet side street where he had an unobstructed view of the Peterson household. Any private investigator worth his salt could not have positioned himself better.

He glanced at his watch. Twenty minutes had passed since he first arrived and still he was frozen to his seat as tightly as a kid's tongue to an icicle.

A light flicked on inside the household followed by another. If he was hoping there was no one home, thereby giving him reason to postpone his decision, he was out of luck.

He was about to reach for the door handle when two distant headlights appeared in his rearview. Steadily the orbs grew larger, suddenly turning spotlight bright, as the driver switched on the vehicle's high beams. Moments later the vehicle slipped into the vacant slot behind him, filling his cab with light.

Unable to determine the type of vehicle or its purpose, he patiently waited for the driver to make the next move. It was not to turn off his lights, however, automatically raising his concern. Eyes locked on the rearview, he noticed a silhouetted figure emerge from the car, walk toward him, and lean his face into the opened driver's side window.

"First rule of surveillance, make sure you keep the object of your attention in front of you," Peterson said.

Adam waited while his boss went back to turn off his lights, kicking himself for his inaction.

"I hope this isn't what it appears to be," Peterson said upon his return, opening the passenger side door and slipping into the seat beside him.

"I was debating whether to come in and see you."

"Social visit?"

"Business."

"Something that can't wait till morning?"

"Yes."

"Something you couldn't tell me over the phone?"

"Yes."

"Must be important," his boss said, rolling down the passenger side window.

Adam reached up and flicked on the cab light, pulled a slip of paper from his shirt pocket, and handed it to his boss.

Peterson unfolded the note and held it to the light. "Let's see," he said, adjusting it to his line of vision. "This is to inform you I am resigning my position effective immediately."

"You were bringing me this?" he asked, lowering the note to his lap.

"Trying to."

His boss leaned back in the seat and spoke as though what just happened didn't happen. "You don't know how many hours I've sat alone like this in a car eyeing somebody's residence," he said. "The toughest thing in the world is to stay awake all night long with nothing to do."

"You mean while on the job?" he asked, somewhat grateful for the postponed reaction to his decision.

"Not only on this job but others. One time I worked the graveyard shift as a fireman for the railroad. This was long after the diesel engines replaced the steam. Once that happened there was no reason for the railroads to keep the firemen around any longer. Why would you when there was no coal to shovel? Featherbedding, they called it. Well, the unions would have nothing of it. They claimed it was a safety issue of the first order, saying the firemen were needed to keep a lookout on the opposite side of the train, watch for the switchmen's signals and relay them to the engineer, which happened maybe once a run. So, you just sat there trying to keep awake, drinking coffee by the barrelful."

"Did you ever get the chance to run one of those things?" he asked, his mind half into the conversation.

"Yes, and that's the irony of it. Every so often one of those old codger engineers would let you run the engine, so he could switch places with you and take a nap in the fireman's seat. Hell, I was hardly old enough to drive a car and there I was at the controls of a train. Believe me, the word spread quickly among the switchmen when they saw it was my head sticking out the engineer's window."

"Started watching their step, huh?"

"Started waving those caution and stop signals to me with their lanterns about a mile before I was to get the thing stopped, just in case."

"Whatever happened to the firemen?"

"The unions and the railroads finally reached a deal. Gave the firemen a nice severance check in exchange for them going away. But you know what, Adam? The trains kept running. The old codgers were up there all alone, but the trains kept running."

"I have to admit there were times when I enjoyed sitting in the military patrol cars alone," Adam said, recalling some of his past experiences.

"Hell, is there anybody you know who doesn't enjoy an occasional sit-alone in their car? For many city people it is the only private space they have in their life. You ever hear of a farmer going out to sit in his truck for some quiet time?"

Adam leaned his head against the headrest. "About that discharge appeal, Pete," he said. He then paused, expecting an objection. Hearing none, he continued. "When I was in Air Force Security, I once received a temporary assignment to a squadron information office. Our entire unit was being transferred to another base, but since I had only three months left in my stint, they decided to give me a desk job to fill out my term. The squadron information officer was the sole person manning the office at the time. He was a second lieutenant straight out of college and on a real power trip. My job was to answer the phone and help out with the paperwork. In other words, I was to serve as his secretary. It didn't take long before I learned that the lieutenant, who was married, had a honey by the name of Melody on the side. It turned out Melody was the civilian employee whose place I had taken. I later learned she had resigned her position on the promise from the lieutenant that he would leave his wife for her. Following her departure and my arrival, the phone calls from her to the lieutenant became a daily thing. When she did call, all business was put on hold while the two engaged in their little love chats and lunch-hour tryst arranging. Meanwhile, I was taking calls from the wife who was wondering where the hell her husband was and why he wasn't returning her calls. In short, I became the official excuse maker, or facilitator, or enabler, take your pick. To make matters worse, the lieutenant's wife happened to be the base commander's niece. Well, it all exploded when the wife discovered the affair and ran to the base commander. These kinds of things are not tolerated in the military, as you might know. As expected, the commander lowered the boom on the information office, charging the lieutenant with conduct unbecoming an officer. I became part of the collateral damage when I was given an Article 15 for dereliction of duty in not reporting the matter, which led to my general discharge."

"And what about Melody?" Pete asked.

"That was the real tragedy of it. There was some overlap between the time I came on board and the time she left. During that period I came to know her a bit. She seemed like a nice enough gal but certainly naïve, as well as a sucker for a guy in uniform. Not to be blasphemous, but I kept thinking "forgive her for she knows not what she does." Many times I wanted to take her by the shoulders and ask flat out "do you know how much of a jerk this guy is?"

"And why didn't you?"

"I was too concentrated on the end game, too busy counting days. I just wanted to get the hell out of there and not be caught up in a nasty situation, so I looked past it all. Besides, what could I do short of ratting him out? Ask for a transfer? I was too much of a short timer for that. But to answer your question, Melody was hung out to dry in the end, literally hung. She was found not long after hanging from a clothes rack in her closet."

"I knew a gal who tried to hang herself in her closet and the whole thing came crashing down on her," Pete interjected. "Gave her a second chance at life and she took it."

"Melody had no second chance and not much of a first chance. I felt like an accomplice of sort," Adam said. "Guilty of moral laxity, if nothing else."

"Melody, Charlene, Eva, quite a lineup," his boss mused aloud, while continuing to ignore the note.

Adam draped his arm out the window. "What made you consider retirement, Pete?"

"The usual things. You start thinking of bodily functions instead of business functions. You think the phone ringing on the television program you're watching is the phone in your living room. Your arms start moving faster than your feet when you are out jogging. Those sorts of signs."

A silent interval between the two ensued as they settled into the still of the night. From a nearby thoroughfare echoes of traffic alternately faded in and out in tandem with the high-pitch hum of cicadas. Above the singsong, came the sound of a siren rising in the distance. Moments later the parting of curtains at the Peterson residence drew their attention, as Jill Peterson glanced out a front window to the street.

"My wife worries about me," his boss said. "It's one of the nice things in life. A necessary thing, I should say. It's something you don't want to forget in case you are planning on going it alone, Adam."

He glanced at the note still clutched in his boss's hand. "About the resignation, Pete. I think it's best. You can call Wheeler first thing in the morning and tell him you've gotten rid of me, before he lowers the hammer. You can explain to him it was all my doing. I think he'll be more than happy to drop the matter once you do."

"I wouldn't be so sure of that," he replied. "So what are you planning on doing, hooking up with a rental cop agency? Going back to watching buildings?"

"It's an option. And also concentrating on my studies—learning the business before I dive headlong into something I have no business getting into."

"What's your teacher's opinion of this move?" he asked.

It was one of the reasons for his indecision. He had yet to even consider the consequences of jumping ship on her, simply due to the press of time. Still, she had every right to know he was planning on bailing out. Otherwise, his bargain with her would go down as another grand example of his starting something without finishing it.

"She doesn't know. I wanted to tell you first," he said. "However, I'm certain she'll agree it's not a bad idea to concentrate on my education first."

The wail of the emergency vehicle drew closer and louder, commanding their attention. It exited the thoroughfare and entered the side road leading to the complex, its rotating lights clearly visible over the tops of cars. Silently and apprehensively, they sat and watched its approach, neither one of them acknowledging its presence until it passed into the night.

"Another retirement sign," his boss muttered, before turning to face him. "You say you want an education, Adam? The best kind you can get in life?"

"Yes, of course," he replied without hesitation.

Peterson took the note in his hand, carefully tore it into pieces, and reached over to stuff it back into the shirt pocket from where it came. "Then I'll see you in the morning," he said. "Right now, I have to go inside. I said my wife worries about me. Actually, she's worried about the groceries in my car. I need to get them in before they spoil."

He watched his boss stroll back to his car, haul out two bulky plastic bags, and saunter off to his villa, his shoulders slightly stooped. Observing him, he was sure of one thing. It wasn't the groceries his wife was worried about when she peered out the window. It was her husband. As for Adam he was glad Pete was still his boss.

CHAPTER TEN

It was a day the winds blew gently over the central city, enabling the aromas of blooming frangipani, cigars, and coffee to mix and mingle, forming a scent as rich and exotic as the legend of the area's patron pirate Gasparilla. It also served as a balm to Adam's worries as he ventured from the office for his trek to the Southside Shopping Plaza. Peterson had come in early to cover for him, saying he could make up the time another day. It was not the most optimistic of sendoffs, the hangover from the previous day's pre-strike warning from the *Beacon* reporter weighing around his boss's neck like the proverbial lodestone. As a precautionary move, he first swung around to Bayshore Boulevard, instinctively checking his rearview to make sure he wasn't being tailed. Weeks may have removed himself from the picture, but it was not beyond Wheeler to sic another hired hand on him.

For several blocks he cruised the bustling boulevard, its scenic, sea-hugging sidewalk filled with strollers, joggers, roller bladers, and young mothers pushing baby carriages. Confident there was no one on his tail, he turned back to the interstate to join the stream of traffic headed south.

In short order he was navigating the bridge approach and toll plaza, powering his pickup toward the crest of the Skyway, its soaring twin cable towers clearly visible on the horizon. Off to his right, the great expanse of the Gulf burst into view, its luminous turquoise waters advancing in rhythmic swells toward shore. Running parallel to the bridge was the old Skyway, its missing southbound center span a stark reminder of the terrible events of not so long ago that continued to haunt to this day.

A short distance past the bridge he came upon the shopping plaza, exiting the interstate and guiding his truck to a stop at the north end of the parking lot. He paused a minute, pulling the *Gazette* reporter's checklist from his shirt pocket to measure it against the lineup of stores. The copy center was located near the far end of the strip but he decided to go ahead and begin his checking on the north end with the thought in mind of saving the best chance for last.

His first stop was the yogurt shop where a bone-thin redhead took the photo of Wheeler from his hand to observe it close-up for a moment. "Nope, don't recognize him," she snipped, handing it back. "Can't say I did," a chunky man donned in a smudge-marked apron said from behind the deli counter. "No, but there was a man here that day asking about a young woman," said an elderly lady at the flower shop. The souvenir shop was next, pieces of scrimshaw among the items prominently displayed in its window. "No, didn't see him," the clerk said, eyeing the photo. Similar responses awaited him down the line at the pizza place, cleaners, and travel agency. As the stores dwindled down, so did his hopes, though the sight of the copy center resurrected them a bit. Entering, he spotted two floppy-haired young men clothed in khakis, white dress shirts, and blue ties working the room, flitting between machines and customers. He waited patiently near the front entrance until the taller of the two finished with a customer and turned his attention to him.

"Can I help you?" he asked, jingling a large ring of keys from his hand.

As with the others, he simply identified himself as a private investigator on a routine missing person search. "Have you seen this fellow in here?" he asked, holding up the newspaper clipping with the photo.

"Nope," the clerk said, without taking the clipping from his hand.

"Sure?"

"Sure."

"What about your co-worker?" he asked, motioning across the room.

"Hey Freddie! Can you come here a minute?" he called to his colleague.

Freddie took the photo in hand and examined it. "No, never seen him."

"Were you both working the day of May ninth?"

The shorter clerk reached out and grabbed a desk calendar for them to check. Eyeing the date they both nodded a yes.

"Thanks," he said.

He exited the store, stopping outside and taking a deep breath to exhale his frustration and settle his mind. The consequences of coming up empty on his search weighed on his mind, as he stepped into the computer store—his final stop. A genial, middle-aged man with a sizable girth and dome top was there to greet him.

"Sorry, I don't recognize the guy," he said when queried. "In all honesty, however, I wasn't working that afternoon."

"Who was?" he asked, looking about the store to see if anyone else was on board.

"Clifford was, but he's not on duty right now. He should be back in about a half hour. He had to run an errand. Would you like to wait for him?'

He waged an internal debate whether it was worthwhile to wait around. "I'll be back," he finally said.

He retraced his steps back down the strip's walkway, stopping at a pay phone adjacent to the souvenir shop. He lifted the phone from its cradle and dialed Peterson.

"Yeah, Pete, wanted to let you know I'm about ready to head back," he said.

"Any luck?"

"None."

"Got a couple of developments on this end," his boss said.

"Yeah?"

"Received a call from Merkel. He's stopping by at one o'clock to tie up some loose ends, he says."

"What do you make of it?" he asked, staring at the scrimshaw pieces on display.

"More likely he's here to tighten the noose. If that's the case, he believes we really do have something to hide. I'll let him have his say and go from there."

"And the other item?"

"Got a call from the accident investigators. They found the hit-and-run vehicle, and it was a van. They also picked up the guy who was driving it. Claimed he fell asleep and then panicked. They are going to charge him with vehicular manslaughter. His attorney indicates he is going to plead guilty."

"So, we're talking four to five years for him?"

"Something along those lines. Here's the interesting part. The guy is a part-time cook at guess where?"

"Okay, where?"

"La Veranda."

"Meaning he worked for Steve Brand," Adam said.

"The lawyer he's got is top of the ladder, one the driver sure as hell couldn't afford."

"Four to five years, the guy's getting off easy," Adam said.

"You can't convict a guy on suspicion," Pete replied. "You and I know what his intent was but the fact Eva was nearly half way out in the street when she was swinging open the door of your truck is the kind of mitigating circumstance that gives pause to a prosecutor. Moreover, it would be a real stretch to try and tie the hit and run to the Sunshine Skyway bridge incident. I'm thinking the movers and shakers did not want to let this go to trial where who knows what cans of worms could be opened, so they paid the guy hush money. He'll receive it when he gets out."

"One mover and shaker in particular," Adam said.

"Let's face it, those newspaper guys are as skilled at staying out of the spotlight as they are at shining one," Pete said.

"Thus far," he said.

He bid his boss goodbye, deciding to trek down to the yogurt shop to kill a little time.

"I'll have a small cup of the white chocolate with the carob chips," he said to the redhead who was busy studying a fingernail.

"Do you want the toppings on the top or on the bottom?" she asked in rote fashion.

"Don't toppings go on top?"

She turned her attention from her nail to him. "Some people like their toppings on the bottom."

"Then why call them toppings?"

She shrugged, turning to get his order.

"I'll tell you what," he said half apologetically. "Let's compromise. I'll take half the toppings on the bottom and half on the top."

He consumed the yogurt on a straight-back wooden bench braced against the front of the store, as he entertained thoughts of his boss and his teacher, both of whom might have been a whole lot better off by dismissing his cause in the beginning.

Tossing his empty cup into a waste container, he trudged back down to the computer store to discover the middle-aged guy had left, replaced by a gangly kid with lank blond hair and thick glasses. He took him to be Clifford.

He introduced himself and explained his reason for being there in case the kid's co-worker hadn't.

"I understand you were working here May ninth," he said.

"Sure was," the fellow replied, his thumbs hooked behind red suspenders stretching down the front of his electric blue shirt to the tip of his purple trousers.

He held up the photo. "Ever see this guy in here?"

The kid adjusted his glasses and fixed his gaze on the photo. "Sure have."

Adam's heart jumped to his throat, causing him to clear it. "On that day?"

"Yes…actually it was on that night. We were closed but I was still here, working late to catch up on my homework. The boss lets me use one of the computers to work on my assignments. Can't afford my own."

"So, he actually wasn't inside the store?"

"Don't tell the boss this, but he was. I let him in," he said. "The lights were on and he was knocking on the front door. I went to see what he wanted. Turns out he really was after the services of the copy center next door, but it had closed, so he stopped here. He wanted to know if there was a photocopy machine he could use. He said he only needed to make a single copy."

"You have one?"

"Nope."

"So he left?"

"Nope," he repeated, creating some momentary confusion. He then motioned to him with his arm. "Let me show you something."

He followed the guy to the rear of the store to a computer workstation tucked in a corner.

"See this little gadget here?" he asked, pointing to what looked like a miniature, square skillet positioned next to the computer. "This is one of the latest tech toys to come onto the market. It's called a scanner. It allows you to enter a document or a photo into a computer by scanning it in. Once transferred into the computer and in digital format, it can be printed out. Being the generous person I am, I did just that for the man in your photo—scanned it in and printed him a copy."

Adam mulled it over for a second. "Let me ask you something,

Clifford. Any chance the document is still in the computer?"

"Well…not sure," he said, contemplating the screen. "The boss periodically goes around and cleans out the hard drives. Let's see."

The kid plopped down at the computer and started flailing away at the keyboard, sending commands flickering across the screen, prompting instant flickering back.

"I hope this isn't violating any privacy rules," Clifford said in a tone signaling he could care less. Presently, he seemed more wrapped up in the search than policies and procedures.

Perhaps they lacked the written kind, Adam thought, recalling his boss's pledge to hand him the responsibility of compiling them for the agency.

"As you pointed out, you were officially closed for business," he said in support of the clerk's action. "It means you were acting on your own," he added, remembering what Peterson initially underscored to him in regard to the investigation.

"Man, oh man, it looks like my boss may have purged it," the clerk said, leaning his eyes closer to the screen to follow the codes. "Wait, wait, wait.., here it is."

He feverishly punched in additional commands. A moment later a document appeared on the screen, at which point Adam could have thrown his arms around Clifford and wrapped him in a bear hug, if he had been willing to risk having the cops called on him for unwanted advances. Instead, he marveled at the screen. Lo and behold, there it was, the paternity affidavit, signed by Charlene Gibbs. Missing was the name and signature of the father, but with Clifford as a witness, it was a footprint not to be denied.

"Do you want a printout?" the clerk asked.

"Yes, and can you get a date and time it was entered into the computer shown on it?"

"I should be able to," he said, fingers flying over the keyboard. One final stroke to activate the printer and Clifford leaned back to await the result of his efforts. For a minute the machine hummed its handiwork before falling silent, prompting the clerk to reach around and pluck the copy from the printer tray and hand it over his shoulder to Adam. Taking a final look, he noted the date, May 9, 1987, and time, 11:02 p.m., entered along the top of the copy, putting Monte Wheeler literally and figuratively on the spot.

He held the copy up to the beaming clerk. "Cost?"

"Like I told the gentleman in the photo, there's no price to pay for something as simple as that."

How unaware we are that the simplest of actions can lead to great cost, he mused, slipping the document into his briefcase. We just don't realize it at the time.

*

"During the course of your investigations, do you ever feel you are operating at cross purposes with law enforcement officials?" Merkel asked.

He was following the same line of questioning they had been subjected to at the Chief Deputy Sheriff's hearing, except the *Beacon* reporter was working the script in a more polished manner.

"What exactly do you mean?" Peterson asked, combing his unruly hair with his fingers.

The three sat facing each other in triangular fashion, his boss having positioned himself in a chair to the side of the desk.

"Your purpose is to serve your client. The purpose of law enforcement is to serve the citizenry. They don't always go hand in hand, I'm sure you'll agree."

"I'd like to think we both have the purpose of providing the truth, which serves everyone well, don't you agree?" Peterson asked.

Merkel ignored the return question, pausing to brush his mustache with the eraser end of his pencil. With his scraggly brown hair, ruddy face, cynical eyes, rumpled shirt, and loosened tie, he resembled the stereotypical reporter of old.

"Let me boil it down to the tactical," he said in his gravel voice. "Have you ever misrepresented yourself in order to gain access to official records?"

"No," Peterson said straight out.

"Has your firm ever participated in corporate espionage cases?"

Peterson reacted to the question like a prizefighter who when hit with a solid overhand right pretends it was little more than a glancing blow.

"There is a difference between investigating and spying," he answered.

The reporter leaned back in his chair and studied them both.

"How about you, Mr. Fraley?" he asked, shifting his eyes in his direction. "Any misrepresentation on your part—for example, passing yourself off as an insurance claims agent or an official family representative?"

"No to the first," he said. "As for the second, I have to ask, is a family claiming I misrepresented them?"

Merkel again ignored the return fire as he checked his notes. "As the nuns once taught me, there are sins of commission and sins of omission," he said. "I suppose the withholding of information would fall into the latter category, when it comes to law enforcement investigations. Is this the way you see it in your business?"

Every time Merkel started constructing a question, Peterson snatched his water bottle, unscrewed the cap, downed a mouthful, and recapped it. His demeanor left little doubt he was becoming restless with the questions, even regretting his decision to entertain them in the first place. Adam considered grace under fire his boss's trademark. He now wondered whether it had reached its expiration date.

"I'm not sure I would categorize it as a sin," Peterson responded, continuing the dance.

Merkel persisted. "Let me put it to you directly. In certain circumstances do you choose to withhold information from law enforcement authorities during the course of an investigation?"

Oh, how Peterson must be tempted, he thought. Here was the opportune time to pull the paternity affidavit out of the hat, slide it across the desk, say politely here's a piece of information we've uncovered, explain the circumstances of it, and then sit back and revel in his reaction. That was the original plan after he rushed back from the shopping plaza to announce the good news. However, in a last-minute reconsideration, they decided to hold the document in reserve. Handing it over to an investigative reporter the caliber of Merkel ensured the path he had traveled to Ohio would be traveled again, this time by the *Beacon* bulldog, with or without the permission of Wheeler. Moreover, he likely would take it a step further, subjecting Charlene Gibbs's child to either public exposure or legal jeopardy once he shined the spotlight on her.

"You're worrying about a kid you've never seen and I'm in a sweat over a business I've been staring in the face for the better part of thirty years," Peterson said to him in their hurried pre-conference. "Now tell me again who has the most to lose?" he asked.

They settled on a compromise, placing one copy of the document in a sealed envelope addressed to Wheeler, agreeing if the noose tightened further, the envelope would go into the nearest mailbox pronto. Another copy was placed in an envelope addressed to the sheriff with the same intent in mind.

"Our general practice is not to withhold information, if legally bound to do otherwise," Peterson replied in answer to Merkel's question.

And on it went, question after question, until Merkel tired of the dance, informing them he had plenty material for a story and besides, he had another appointment to make. No sooner was he out the door than Peterson casually turned to him. "That professor of yours better come through for us," he said, taking another swig of water.

"What was the corporate espionage bit about?" he asked, sensing it touched a nerve.

"He's upping the ante by threatening to drag my wife into the picture."

"In what way?"

Peterson took a deep breath. "Years ago my wife and I had an acquaintance who was an executive recruiter, also known on the street as a headhunter. His job was to scout and recruit top candidates for corporations trying to fill upper level management positions in this region. He acted as sort of a matchmaker between the recruit and the corporation. He made sure his work was carried out in a very confidential manner."

"Who pays the headhunter's fee?" he asked, interrupting Peterson's account to satisfy his curiosity.

"The company doing the hiring pays the headhunter's fee," he said, brushing back loose strands of hair from his forehead. "The reason for the confidentiality is the corporation doesn't want to appear desperate to fill the position and the recruit doesn't want to look like he is job hunting. Anyway, this acquaintance was anxious to make sure his stable of recruits knew exactly what they were getting into before taking the leap. He considered it part of his quality control program. As part of his package, he would offer the recruits what he called an insider's perspective. As he explained it, a recruit can conduct all the paper research on a company he cares to, but it will never provide him an accurate inside look into the actual workplace environment he may be headed into. And he was right. I hear stories all the time, as I'm sure you have, about people who accept new jobs, thinking things look great from the outside but then once on the job find out there is trouble brewing, usually in the form of a power-tripping supervisor. Well, that's where we came into the picture. Our acquaintance had connections with some of the temporary hire services his corporate clients utilized. His idea was to see if he could arrange to have a temporary worker, preferably a secretarial type, from one of the temp firms placed in one of his client corporations. He got the idea from a friend of his who once worked on a federal task force on organized crime. The feds considered trying it on Jimmy Hoffa's organization, if you can believe it. They wanted to plant a temp in his office instead of a bug. They lined up a female agent for the job, manufactured her a fat resume, and were about to land her a job there under one of Hoffa's underlings when higher ups pulled the plug on the operation."

"Scary thing to be called a temporary worker in a Jimmy Hoffa operation," he said, jumping into his boss's narrative.

"Yeah, for sure," he said with a wan smile. "So anyway, in our little operation, the secretary, after working there a short while, was to report to the headhunter and his executive recruit on the internal status of the firm, briefing them on any major troubles brewing in the place before the recruit accepted the position."

"Not wanting him or her to walk into a hornets nest," he volunteered.

Peterson leveled a finger at him. "Exactly. There were a couple of reasons the headhunter came to us. First, we were in the investigating business. Secondly, my wife had secretarial experience. Who better to give an opinion on the internal dynamics of a company than an observant executive secretary?"

"Who was responsible for her pay?" he asked, in the same breath realizing he was displaying an unusual interest in who was paying whom.

"She received the temp salary and the Peterson Private Investigation Agency received a cut of the fee paid to the headhunter. A typical fee for filling a high-level executive position is one-third of the recruit's first year's pay, which for an executive earning a hundred and fifty thousand a year comes out to fifty thousand. Of that fifty thousand, we received five percent or twenty-five hundred. This was on top of the regular temp salary my wife received. It was nice money and we needed it at the time to help make a down payment on our villa."

"How did it work out?" he asked, sensing something was out of kilter.

"It lasted for two recruits. Actually, everything went fine as far as the planning went. My wife signed up with the temp agency the headhunter recommended and soon was working as a temporary executive secretary for a couple of firms on his list. In both cases she gave an oral report to the headhunter and recruits following her assignments. The problem was my wife felt like a snitch. From a legal standpoint there was really nothing wrong with it. She wasn't into pilfering documents or anything of the sort. Nor was she breaking any confidentiality rules. All she was doing was giving her impression of what it was like working there, just as any other employee might do."

"Why couldn't he have sought out the opinions of employees already working at these places?"

Peterson shook his head. "It's not the same. They are less likely to spill the beans to strangers, plus they are not privy to the major problems that may be boiling beneath the surface at the higher echelons."

"So how do you suppose Merkel got wind of your arrangement?"

"I'm guessing this acquaintance of ours was rubbing shoulders with the movers and shakers on a daily basis and probably couldn't keep his mouth shut during a bragging session following a couple of cocktails."

"Maybe at La Veranda?"

"Could well be where Wheeler picked it up. I know it was one of this guy's favorite hangouts."

"If there is nothing illegal about it, why the concern, Pete?"

"Oh, there may be ethical issues involved, if not legal ones. But what the hell isn't in our business? As you know by now, Adam, we toe these lines every day," he said, tapping his fingers nervously on the desk. "Is there any story easier to slant for a hit piece than this? All you have to do is pound home the spy word. I can see it now: Private investigator sends out wife to spy on corporate office employees."

"It hardly ranks as page-one stuff," Adam said, trying to ease his boss's anxiety.

"Yeah, but when they throw it into the mix with everything else, it becomes combustible. The bad part is now I have to go home and let my wife know what could be coming," he said, hurling an empty bottle into the waste container. "Smearing my reputation is one thing; smearing hers is another. I swear, if I see her name on the front page of the paper, I'll go down and shoot the son of a bitch."

He wasn't sure whether he was referring to Merkel or Wheeler but was not about to ask for a clarification.

"Do you want to switch plans and play the affidavit?" Adam asked, realizing the stakes had been raised dramatically.

"Nah," his boss said. "Let's stick to the game plan. He wants us to fold, suspecting we might hold the better hand. Maybe your teacher friend will send him a message he could be right in thinking so."

"We do have an alternative, you know. Instead of the affidavit, we could fire off a copy of the Hilltop Inn parking lot incident report to Wheeler and Ward Fletcher," he said. "It may ensure he doesn't rest easy in his new life, knowing the sheriff may be looking over his shoulder."

"What gave you that idea?"

"A line from my Shakespeare class: 'uneasy lies the head that wears the crown.' In other words, 'uneasy lies the head that weds the sheriff's niece.' The report would put Fletcher on notice as to what kind of a guy his niece is married to. In a way we would be doing a public service, exposing a batterer, if not a philanderer. The downside is the report again raises the risk of eventually drawing Charlene's child into the picture."

Peterson shook his head. "The chances of a link being made between the parking lot incident and the child are slim, unless somehow Wheeler divulges it, and that isn't going to happen. I say put the parking lot report in with the affidavit and hold it in reserve until we see how things play out. And by the way, the next time you bring back a quote from school, could you make it one from your criminology class or else I'm going to start believing you are preparing to jump ship on the profession."

"Okay, here you go, one of the fundamental principles of criminology as stated by our instructor," he said, immediately taking up the suggestion. 'There's a reason for every human act, even if the action is ultimately deemed by law to be unreasonable.'"

Peterson creased his brow and touched his temple with a forefinger. "As if I didn't already have a headache," he said. "Back to the crown-on-the-head thing. I take it old Will is referring to the great responsibility of a king, right?"

"Among other things, right."

"Well, this is my kingdom," he said, his eyes circling the room, his finger jabbing the air. "It may not rate up there with the responsibility of a king, but who's to say a king's responsibility means more to him than this little kingdom does to me?"

His boss stood and grabbed his jacket. "I've got to run. I have an appointment over at the Port Authority."

"Your wife finally talk you into a cruise?" he asked.

"You could say that. By the way, I may be out and about the next couple of days taking care of some business in case you don't hear from me," he said, hurrying out the door.

*

Weaving in and out of traffic streams, Adam glanced at his watch as he headed back across town to the *Gazette* building. According to Miss Egan's secretary, he still had time to catch her before she left for the day, since it appeared she would be tied up in a board meeting for a while longer. Finding the building was no problem, having passed it on numerous occasions through the years. At one time it served as a post office processing and distribution center, prior to being taken over and renovated by the Gazette Corporation. A two-story, white-stucco structure, it offered a strictly functional appearance in contrast to the bedrock institutional look of the *Beacon* building.

He eased into the parking lot, noting her Mustang sitting in a section reserved for management. Inside, a bubbly receptionist escorted him down a fluorescent-lit hallway, past glass-paneled advertising and administrative offices to a ballroom-sized newsroom with partitioned workstations. "Her desk is at the far end," she said, gesturing down a narrow aisle.

Miss Egan's eyes widened with surprise at the sight of him. "Have a chair," she said, rising to greet him from behind a tidy desk.

She was wearing a champagne-colored blouse and pleated plaid skirt, a fashion falling somewhere between the formality of her classroom and informality of her parlor room. He wanted to tell her right off how terrific she looked but thought better of it.

"What brings you out this way?" she asked.

"Breaking news."

"It must be the good kind. There's a joyful look about you."

"Maybe it's from seeing you," he blurted out, wishing to God he hadn't.

She held her expression. "I'm thinking there must be something else at play."

He dug a copy of the affidavit out of his briefcase and passed it across the desk. Her reaction on reading it was to slightly raise an eyebrow and lay it aside next to a framed photograph of a distinguished-looking older man he hoped was her father.

"Nice work," she said. "How did it come into your possession?"

"I followed in the footsteps of your reporter."

"The father's name is missing," she pointed out.

"I know, but the date and time, as well as a witness I found, places him on the bridge."

She picked the document back up and held it aloft. "My copy?"

"Yes. I thought you might want to see it before you wrote your article."

"It's already written," she said.

"It's going to run as is?" he asked, wondering if the affidavit would warrant changes.

Again she set the document aside. "As is, as of now."

He noted a twinge of uncertainty in her voice. "You sound as if there may be a hitch."

"Our publisher received a call from Mr. Wheeler," she said directly.

It came as no surprise to Adam. "When you feel you have a complaint, go directly to the top," he said. "Isn't that what the experts always recommend?"

"He's pulling no punches," she said. "He brought up the matter of my applying for his former position at the *Beacon* and my being turned down for it. He's claiming I am carrying out some sort of personal vendetta against him as a result."

"The publisher was unaware of your interest in the job?"

"Yes, he was unaware. If I had chosen to remain in the running instead of withdrawing my name from consideration, I would have notified him of my intent. Unless you are among the final candidates for an outside job, I've never felt you had an obligation to notify your superiors. Otherwise you may be creating a lot of unnecessary concern in the workplace, something I chose not to do."

"I take it Wheeler did not mention you withdrawing your name from consideration."

"No, and he also didn't mention the breach of confidentiality he was committing in notifying my publisher of my application for the position."

"How deep into the details did he get?"

"If you mean the deepest details, not deep at all. He's betting on the job search issue and even more so on his father having been a friend of our publisher."

"How good a friend?"

"From what I understand, it was more of a professional friendship. His father was also in the publishing business, mainly magazines. I suspect it is one reason why his son reached his lofty position. Naturally, there was a competitiveness between the two publishers, but also a sense of 'we're in this business together' and any external attack on one should be considered an attack on the other," she said. "These people constantly rub shoulders at cocktail parties. They are not above asking favors of each other, especially if it involves family."

Sort of like what Peterson did with Ronnie Weeks, mentioning Katie, he thought.

"Is Wheeler's father still alive?"

"He died several years ago."

"Which way is your publisher leaning? Any idea?"

"As I mentioned, he currently is in the process of mulling it over. In our preliminary discussion, he raised the idea of delaying the story to give the lawyers more time to review it. He did ask why I did not give a courtesy call to Mr. Wheeler."

"Courtesy call?"

"Yes…a heads up the story was coming."

"Is that normal protocol?"

"It is when a story centers on a certain person whom you quote extensively. The story I wrote is not about Wheeler, however. It's about Charlene Gibbs and the two tragedies that vaulted her story into the public domain. In my opinion a courtesy call was out of the question and could even be interpreted as setting a bad precedent. From the publisher's perspective, it may have been appropriate, but that's where we differ."

Her response raised in him an obvious hypothetical question. "Suppose Wheeler had no personal relationship with Charlene and still asked you to kill the story out of respect for the family?"

She narrowed her eyes in disapproval. "Let me turn the question back at you. Suppose you discovered during the course of your investigation there was no personal relationship between the two, would you still want me to do the story?"

He pondered the question for a moment. "Okay, I confess my

enthusiasm would have been dampened considerably."

"Fortunately or unfortunately, it's the way journalists often view the world. They see a story first and a personal tragedy second, while you see it as just the opposite. Who's to say in the end we are not both right?"

The optimism he arrived with had given way to a sobering reality. Someone's truth can be another man's burden.

"How are you coming along with your assignment?" she asked, relieving him of his thought.

"I was afraid you might ask. I—"

"Miss Egan, Mr. Jordan would like to see you."

They turned in unison to see a shaggy-haired youngster leaning his head into the doorway, his eyes appearing like balloons behind his shot-glass thick spectacles.

"Thanks, Roger. Tell him I'm on my way."

She reached for her handbag. "I have to run. Mr. Jordan is the publisher. He hung around after the board meeting to go over my article."

"How great a chance is there he will kill it?" Adam asked.

"There's always a chance, but I'm a fairly persuasive person, especially when it comes to this story."

"Does he make it a practice of overruling you?"

"No, it's not common of him," she said, adopting a reassuring tone.

"Should I stick around for the verdict?"

"Are you asking if you should or if you can?"

"What do you think?"

"I think you should go home and relax. You've done all you can. It's out of your hands now."

He accepted her advice and rose to leave.

"Adam," she said to his back in her parlor voice, stopping him in his tracks. "I'll see you in class."

He turned to her, fearing the look of joy on his face was no doubt on display again. "See you, Miss Egan."

*

Try as he might, he was unable to focus on females in male locker rooms, not when his mind was preoccupied with the clock on his mantel whose hands circled at a cruel pace clear through to Sunday morning. As was his morning habit, he threw on a pair of jeans and t-shirt and strolled down the block from his apartment complex to a corner bakery to pick up a couple of bagels, cream cheese, and coffee. On his return he purchased copies of the *Sunday Gazette* and *Beacon* from a phalanx of vending machines outside the store, fighting the temptation to take a peek at their contents before reaching the comfort and privacy of his living room. Once settled in, he leafed through the Beacon first, scanning the headlines and bylines for Wheeler's preemptive strike. Relieved he had not beaten them to the punch, he turned to the *Gazette*, spreading it across his coffee table. Briefly, he eyed the page-one headlines, before leafing to the front page of the local section where next to a photo taken at night of the floodlit Skyway Bridge ran a headline streaming nearly half way across the page.

Sisters follow same tragic path—

Nancy Egan, City Editor

When Charlene Gibbs leaped to her death from the Sunshine Skyway Bridge on the night of May 9, it marked a double tragedy for the Gibbs' family. Seven years earlier to the day, on May 9, 1980...

Her rural upbringing...her move to the city...her sister's death...her return home...her devoted parents' deaths...everything worth leaving in, she left in. Everything worth leaving out, she left out, including the personal relationship between Wheeler and Charlene and the child resulting from it. Early on in the story she slipped in the fact that Charlene was "the sister-in-law of *Bay Area Beacon* Executive Editor Monte Wheeler," and left it at that, a tidbit to the general public, a time bomb to Wheeler's professional colleagues. "Why didn't we get this story?" undoubtedly would be the first question raised by someone at the top of the *Beacon* echelon, one Wheeler would have great interest in seeing squelched. There may not have been a crime committed, but it wouldn't take a judge to decree an injustice had been done, if the truth somehow should surface.

He kicked off his shoes, stretched his legs out on the couch, crossed them at his ankles, and finished his bagels and coffee, his thoughts confined to the immediate aftermath of events. In time he drifted into a sleep, broken abruptly by the ringing of the phone.

"What do you think?" his boss asked right off, unable to contain the glee in his voice.

"I think she did good," Adam said, attempting to wake to the moment.

"Ditto. Tell her so for me."

"I'll do that."

"You sound under-whelmed, like you got postpartum depression or post-traumatic syndrome, one of those things," Peterson said, sounding more like his old self.

"I'm now thinking it may not be enough, Pete," he said. "It may give him pause but not put him in his place, if you know what I mean."

"Well, how about me telling you another boating story that's sure to cheer you up."

"With flying fish in it."

"No fish in this one," his boss said. "Can you drop by the house? I've got something to show you."

"Right now?"

"Right now."

*

By early afternoon he was back home, still trying to absorb the impact of the morning's events. He called his teacher to congratulate her on the article and pass along the results of his latest confab with his boss. He then hopped from his couch and marched out the front door, climbing into his rental truck to set off on a Sunday morning drive. Aimlessly, he cruised the streets from

Ybor City to Hyde Park, at one point passing one of those spontaneous flower-draped crosses positioned alongside a road to commemorate a loved one's untimely death. A sign of misplaced devotion, he believed, yet the sight of it was enough to set him off on a return trip to the Skyway.

In quick order he traveled to and over the causeway leading to the bridge. On clearing the southbound span, he glanced to his right toward the old broken Skyway with its missing center span, as much a magnet to the passing eye as the graceful arch of the new bridge.

He exited at the shopping plaza to make a U-turn. Driving past the stores, his attention was drawn to the computer shop where his patience had been rewarded days earlier. Completing the U-turn, he headed back toward the Skyway, paying the bridge toll a second time. He then drove the northbound span to the spot that first led him on his current path.

Clear of traffic he once more steered his truck to a stop in the emergency lane. Immediately, he jumped from the pickup, a rush of tangy salt air blowing in off the gulf greeting him on his exit. Checking traffic, he loped across the lane to the bridge railing. Leaning against the barrier, he gazed for several minutes at the serene waters, as though an explanation for the strange combination of exuberance and melancholy mushrooming within him would come bubbling to the surface at any moment. Suddenly, the din of a powerful engine echoed deep within the hollow of the bridge, breaking his spell. Below him, the bow of an inbound freighter burst into view, followed by its cargo deck and wheelhouse. He followed the trail of the ship as it churned clear of the bridge, a flock of seagulls skimming low in its wake.

With the passing of the ship, calm returned to the bay, the sun's reflection off its shimmering surface nearly blinding him. He momentarily closed his eyes, blocking out the sight but not the sounds.

"Mr. Fraley, we meet again," a voice called out from behind

him.

It came as no great surprise. When passing the shopping plaza earlier, he could not help but notice the late model Jaguar parked in front of the computer store.

He glanced over his shoulder to the approaching figure. "Yeah, all roads seem to lead back to this spot."

"If I didn't know better, I'd say destiny drove us here," Wheeler said, drawing to his side. "Kid at the computer shop is much too accommodating. He said he was only trying to help you out the day you dropped into his store"

"Customer-friendly I think is the term," Adam said.

"Nice feature article in the paper today," Wheeler said, attempting to maintain a neutral tone. "I should have hired the woman when I had the chance. She sure knows how to neuter a guy."

"Neuter or neutralize?" he asked.

"Both."

He glanced around to see the Jaguar parked in front of his truck in the emergency lane.

"Rental car?" Adam asked, unable to resist the jab.

"Not today," he replied. "But I do like yours."

The two were leaning their frames against the guardrail, fixing their gazes directly below.

"Did you know it's best for jumpers to make the leap from further down the center span? That way they are sure to hit the water and not the rocks at the base of the pier down there," Wheeler said.

"A nice tip to give someone you know is going to jump," he replied.

"What do you think, Fraley? Is suicide an act of courage or a coward's way out?" the editor asked. "I'd be interested in your opinion."

His stomach clenched. "I suppose it depends on one's frame of mind at the time," he said. "But don't let me stand in your way."

Wheeler chuckled. "Careful what you say, Fraley. You don't want to destabilize someone in a bad frame of mind who's standing next to a bridge railing."

"Something *you* would never do, of course," Adam said, turning to face him directly.

Wheeler gave him a lopsided grin. "This bridge has brought me nothing but bad luck with women," he said.

"I'd say better luck next time but I understand the next time has already arrived for you," he said, returning his gaze to the water. "How's the wife?"

"She's fine, thank you for asking," he said in mock civility. "We're seriously thinking of starting a family. And by the way, you might be relieved to know she travels this bridge with no trepidation whatsoever."

Cars whisked by behind them in staccato bursts of energy, their drivers oblivious to the two figures who were in turn oblivious to them.

"What's the motive here, Fraley—your motive?" Wheeler asked above the din. "You trying to impress your boss? Most guys would have passed her by in the same situation, maybe settled for a wolf whistle to satisfy their momentary lust."

"It's not a what, it's a who," he said, having finally arrived at an answer. "My father once said to me 'don't do anything in your life you'll later regret on your deathbed.'"

"Tough standard your father set. I would think deathbed considerations would be far removed from someone your age."

"When my father spoke of regrets, he wasn't talking about stock portfolios you've accumulated, jobs you've worked, houses you've lived in, automobiles you've owned, or vacations you've taken. They are not the thoughts of a dying man. He was speaking of the people who give direction to your life."

"Like a lone woman sitting on a bridge railing late at night," Wheeler said, as if it failed to meet the deathbed standard.

"Unfortunately, the lone woman sitting on the rail had the bad fortune of spending the same time on earth as you," Adam said, drawing a quick glare from Wheeler. "Looking forward to work tomorrow?" he added.

"It may not be as bad as you think, Fraley. I've built up my share of credits in the organization, not to mention a boatload of IOUs. It's the kind of stuff not easily dismissed by the hierarchy. The way I look at it, you and I come out of this in a stalemate—a tie, so to speak. You should be grateful, as should your boss."

"I've always been under the impression—"

The blast of a horn from a passing truck punctured the steady drone of traffic behind them, as motorists maneuvered in and out of lanes.

"—I've always been under the impression when you enter a contest as the favorite and come out tied, you're the loser," Adam said, completing his thought.

"Like much of what you see in life, it depends on how you frame it," Wheeler said. "Like I said, you should feel grateful as is. After all, what have you got for all your efforts? An unsigned affidavit from a mentally distressed woman? A rental car record with no bridge tape to back it up? Maybe another minor tidbit or two in reserve? And you were hoping to pin a criminal charge on me with those? By the way, you also may be interested to know I am a regular patron of our favorite computer store. The staff is new, so it's no surprise they would not readily recognize me. I've made a number of business-related purchases there over the years and have always made a point of keeping my receipts for tax purposes. The fact I stopped by there on the day in question, even at an odd hour, is not all that unusual."

"Maybe I'm carrying a wire," Adam quipped.

Wheeler gave him his best smirk. "I doubt that, since you were not expecting to see me. Besides, have I confessed to anything that places me by her side at the time she leaped? I can't tell you how many times young reporters have rushed into my office thinking they have a scoop on their hands when if they had only taken a step back to consider what it was they actually had, they would have realized it was the equivalent of what you have, little or nothing. Apparently, Mr. Fraley, you have as much to learn about the private eye business as you do the journalism profession. Hasn't that boss of yours taken the time to share any of his wit and wisdom with you? Or am I wrong in thinking he has no wit or wisdom to begin with? Pardon my personal editorial, but the guy strikes me as a dunderhead."

Adam shrugged. "Well, he did share a bit of professional knowledge with me earlier today, which I'm sure he wouldn't mind me passing on to you."

"Having to do with what?"

"Having to do with your good fortune of escaping the bridge cameras on the night in question. I'm sure they were not on your mind in the heat of the moment. Once you were notified of her death and told there were no witnesses other than me, you probably held your tongue, hoping nothing would show up on the tapes. Otherwise you would have had to fall back on the lame claim she was alive when you left her."

"This is insight from your boss?" Wheeler mockingly asked in return. "Sounds like more conjecturing to me. You are beginning to sound like one of those electronic media people who seem to think there is no escaping the eye of the camera, that it is about to replace the mind's eye of the print media. This entire episode should show you just how unreliable the camera can be compared to this," he said, pointing to a gloating eye.

Adam casually leaned back from the railing to glance up and down the span. "Unless, of course, they are working in tandem," he said. "It doesn't require any conjecturing to realize the new Skyway is a big attraction. Lately, Peterson's wife has been trying to talk him into taking a cruise with her, specifically a day-tripper out of the Port of Tampa, one that would take them under the bridge at night. Apparently, her friends have been telling her what a spectacular sight it is, seeing the Skyway from down below when it is lit up like a stage in the sky."

Wheeler's expression reflected a newfound interest in what Adam was saying, the mask of confidence having lifted, replaced by a look of concern.

"Chances are you were not aware of the small inbound cruise ship that cleared the bridge the night Charlene stood here," Adam continued. "I never made much of it myself, even when I mentioned it to my boss in a recent rehash we had of the event. I told him it was maybe a few hundred yards into the bay the moment I noticed it—"

"Get on with it, Fraley," Wheeler snapped, his hair flapping in the wind. "What does this have to do with anything?"

"It has to do with everything," he said. "Peterson checked for the name of the ship at the port. It turned out to be chartered to a travel group from over in Orlando. Twenty-eight people were aboard. During its inbound passage, many of the passengers gathered on the rear deck for the highlight of their trip—a grand photo shoot. They were armed with telephoto cameras and camcorders, the late-model kind with night vision capabilities. You can imagine the treasure trove of film they came back with. Being the persuasive guy he is, Peterson managed to get a list of the passengers and proceeded to contact them, asking if they would be willing to share their shots of the bridge. As luck would have it, several segments of video film footage and a couple of still shots show a woman standing near the railing. I don't need to tell you who it was. Seconds later, a man shows up at her side in two other shots as well as in another video. He appears to exchange words with her before disappearing. But here's where we got it wrong. There was a third person in the car that night, the one who shows up by her side at the guardrail in the tapes and photos—Steve Brand."

Wheeler fell into full mute mode, letting him continue his story uninterrupted.

"I'm guessing you were behind the wheel when things got

heated, so much so Charlene either was booted from the car or let out when she demanded it. While you simmered in the car, Brand took off after her for some reason, maybe in anger to tell her to go ahead and jump. During his exchange with Charlene, he jerks his head back toward the road, as if someone is calling to him, probably you yelling at him to get back in the car. It all seemed pretty innocent to the passengers observing it through their lenses from the dark far below, just another couple of passersby, perhaps tourists, stopping to take a hurried peek at the bay. By the time I arrived on the scene the boat had traveled on and the passengers' cameras were directed elsewhere. And thanks to the minimal media coverage, none of them were aware of what transpired minutes later, a testament to your ability to keep the public uninformed."

The roar of a transport truck behind them brought a temporary halt to his narrative.

"It's clear now it was Brand, not one of your police sources, who tipped you off to my snooping," Adam said immediately on the heels of the truck's passing. "The moment I told him I was doing a profile on Charlene for the family, he knew it was bogus, since he had to be aware she had no family left. And since I first spoke to you after I had spoken to him, it means the surprise I thought I was springing on you in your office came as no surprise at all, despite your display of indignation. Right?"

He paused to await a response. There was none.

"What was it, Wheeler? After your wife was killed did your sister-in-law suddenly become one of the favors to be passed around at La Veranda? It must have been easy for her boss and brother-in-law to turn her into a plaything, considering her mental state. I'm guessing Brand provided the playpen, which explains what you were doing south of the bridge. Turns out, he owns a villa there. If I had to guess further, I'd say the confrontation among you three stretched all the way from Brand's home to the bridge with a stopover at the computer shop. Why you wanted to make a copy of the form I'm not sure. It may have been a move to calm her. As for *who* the father might be, I don't know and do not care, though all signs point to you. At this stage Pete and I have decided to let the authorities sort it all out. That is why the pertinent portions of the tapes and photos are on their way to the sheriff's office, along with the other supporting documents we were holding—our minor tidbits, as you refer to them."

It was enough to end Wheeler's silence. "If all of what you say is true, Fraley, need I point out the obvious. It is Brand you have on film, not me."

"Yes, but do you really want to throw a guy under the bus who knows what skeletons are hidden in whose closets, a guy who can come up with a lackey at a moment's notice to do an unconscionable roadside hit, even if done without your knowledge.

Wheeler looked at him long and pointedly. "Feeling good are you, Fraley?"

"Feeling like I just delivered a message from the dead letter file," Adam said.

The editor held his glare. "For you to act like it was some kind of major crime in the first place is the most bewildering aspect of this story."

"As you media people like to point out, the cover-up is oftentimes worse than the original crime, if by chance it is determined to be one."

Adam leaned his forearms on top of the railing. and looked out over the expanse of the bay. "Sounds to me like it might be a good topic for an investigative piece," he said.

Wheeler appeared in no mood to rush off, doubtlessly taking the time to curse his bad luck. Gradually, as though resigned to circumstance, he slowly pushed himself away from the guardrail and marched back to his car.

Adam lingered a while longer to give his mind time to settle, fending off thoughts of what he might have done or said differently from Melody to Charlene to Eva. Second-guessing was second nature to him, perhaps not such a bad thing for a relative newcomer to the profession.

"Sir, Sir!" came another voice from behind him, ending his reflection.

He turned from the railing to see a young woman leaning her head out of the passenger-side window of a dark blue sedan. "Do you need help?" she asked.

"No, I'm fine," he called back.

"Are you sure?"

"I'm sure," he replied, sending the sedan on its way. "Thank you for asking," he added almost as an afterthought, his words trailing in the wind.

EPILOGUE

"I'm pleased you could come," the pastor said from his open doorway. "How was the drive?"

"A familiar one," Adam said with a grin.

"I was so pleased you sent me the article on Charlene. It's what led to my invitation of course," he said, as they stepped from his office.

"Are you sure this is appropriate?" he asked.

"Oh yes, entirely so. I cleared it with the parents and the school," the pastor said. "Do you mind driving? My reflexes are not getting any better."

"Not at all," he said, his apprehension turning into anticipation.

"Back in his old pickup, they drove the road to Rocky Point and further north to a town called Middleton where they stopped at a sign announcing Longwood Elementary School.

"From the sound of things, it looks like we made it right on time," he said, nosing his pickup into a vacant parking slot.

"If you don't mind me asking, how did you find her, pastor?"

"Mr. Fraley, after your last visit, I got to thinking that I told you many things I probably shouldn't have. Let's just say it wasn't the hand of God at work."

They followed a sidewalk fronting the one-story yellow brick building to a playground located on the side. Amid the mix of bright red, white and blue swing sets, slides, twisting tunnels, and frolicking children roamed a woman of slight stature and soft features who was monitoring activities with arms folded.

"Morning, Miss Applebaum," the pastor called above the din on their approach, a sure indication this wasn't the pastor's first visit.

"Good morning, Pastor Conroy," she responded cheerfully, extending her arms to give him a welcoming hug.

"Got your hands full, I see," the pastor added.

"Oh yes, for another ten minutes."

"This here is Adam Fraley, the fellow from Tampa I was telling you about," he said, stepping to the side.

She nodded. "Nice to meet you."

"Nice meeting you."

The pastor clasped his hands in front of him in eagerness. "Well, is she here?"

"Follow me," she said.

They trailed her to the far side of the playground where a group of children were lined up single-file alongside a large sunken sandbox. Apparently, they were engaging in some sort of long-jump contest, each taking a turn at a standing jump from the curb of the box into the sand. As soon as they completed the jump, another adult on hand would run up and measure the distance.

"Colleen!" the teacher called to the last girl in line patiently waiting her turn.

She rotated her body around to face them, providing him an instant vision of the past. She wore a baby-blue pullover shirt, cuffed khaki trousers, and scruffy sneakers, not unlike those worn by her classmates. But it was the raven hair and familiar facial features, in particular the clear violet eyes, pure enough to lift the heaviness from any heart, that set her apart. There was no mistaking where they came from.

"Hi Pastor Conroy," she said in a sprite voice, obviously surprised at his appearance.

"Colleen, I'd like for you to meet someone," he said. "This here is Mr. Fraley."

He took a step forward and extended his hand. "Hello Colleen."

She quickly glanced at her teacher and pastor before returning her eyes to him.

"Hi," she said with a smile, taking it.

Adam widened his own smile in response and in a trice released her hand, nodding her back to her game.

They lingered for a few minutes, absorbing the scene until Miss Applebaum grabbed a whistle hanging from her neck and blew the session to a close, sending the children scurrying back to class and

Adam and the pastor on the road home.

*

Adam stopped for his usual visit to his parents, assuring them over dinner and ice cream he was still on track with his education and not to worry. He then broke the good news to them. He had received word his discharge appeal had been approved. "The overall quality of the applicant's service record is more accurately represented by an honorable discharge," the review board concluded. Maybe his boss was right after all in thinking Stan Conley a reasonable man. He was particularly pleased with his father's joyful reaction for it was mainly on his behalf he filed the appeal in the first place. Still, if truth be told, he was not so sure the decision was well deserved. Whether he was an accomplice or innocent bystander in the Melody matter was a debate not likely to be settled with his self anytime soon.

The following morning, fresh from a good night's sleep, he was Tampa-bound. Streaks of pink brightened the horizon, as he turned his attention to the road ahead. There were decisions to be made, now that the bridge incident was behind him. Only a week ago, a front-page notice appeared in the *Beacon*, informing readers the paper's Executive Editor Monte Wheeler was stepping down from his position. Why he was leaving was left vague. A subsequent phone call to the La Veranda was all it took for them to learn Brand was no longer working there. A sure sign a deal had been reached among higher-ups, according to Peterson. All things considered, everyone involved had reason for keeping things quiet, especially the existence of a love child. As a criminal matter, Brand and Wheeler at most may have been subject to involuntary manslaughter charges but, as in the Eva Green case, proof beyond a reasonable doubt would have been difficult. Nonetheless, the consequences for their professional careers, not to mention their personal lives, were an entirely different matter. Whatever the agreement, Wheeler no longer loomed as a threat, enabling Adam's boss to breathe a sigh of relief. Peterson now had the green light to pursue his scrimshaw shop dream.

As part of his retirement planning, Pete at one point raised the notion of selling his business. "Interested in taking this on?" he asked over the desk one morning, knowing full well the matter of finding the investment capital to do so would be an issue for a novice like Adam. "I guarantee you won't have to worry about running out of clients, Adam. This business thrives on a lack of trust in society and there's plenty of that to go around. The country may run out of oil but it will never run out of mistrust," he said. "Count me as a suitor," Adam responded in return, at once surprising and pleasing his boss.

Regarding his academic pursuits, he did manage to finish his journalism class essay, receiving a B for his effort, his teacher telling him the relatively minimal incorporation of the female point of view was the only thing keeping him from a higher grade. As for his sole extra-curricular activity, it had been on hold, placed there by him due to a lack of confidence, or propriety, or both, despite the class having ended. Yet, the images of her lingered on. What was it his boss said about the way a woman like her carries herself? The answer rode home with him, ultimately guiding him to a decision. Both the ownership matter and resumption of classes were weeks away. Meanwhile, he had plenty of time to see if he could get lucky.

Adam pulled his pickup into his drive, sat for a few reflective moments, and then gunned it back out again, swinging it in the direction of Longfellow Lane.

ABOUT THE AUTHOR

Henry Hoffman is a former public library director and newspaper editor whose fiction and non-fiction works have appeared in a variety of literary and trade publication.

He is the author of three previous novels, *Bound, Drums Along the Jacks Fork, and Flaherty's Run.* Along with his works of fiction, he has contributed articles to a number of standard reference works, including *America: History and Life* (ABC-CLIO), the *Encyclopedia of Flight* (Salem Press), *Historical Abstracts of the United States* (ABC-CLIO), and the *Encyclopedia of Natural Disasters* (Salem Press).

www.ingramcontent.com/pod-product-compliance
Lightning Source LLC
Chambersburg PA
CBHW070455260626
47161CB00004B/1313